THE DREAM OF MY RETURN

Horacio Castellanos Moya

THE DREAM OF MY RETURN

TRANSLATED FROM THE SPANISH
BY KATHERINE SILVER

A NEW DIRECTIONS PAPERBOOK ORIGINAL

Published by arrangement with Horacio Castellanos Moya
and his agent and publisher, Tusquets Editores, Barcelona.

Originally published in Spain as *El sueño de mi retorno* by Tusquets Editores.

Manufactured in the United States of America
New Directions Books are printed on acid-free paper.
First published as a New Directions Paperbook (NDP1301) in 2015

Library of Congress Cataloging-in-Publication Data
Castellanos Moya, Horacio, 1957–
[Sueño del retorno. English]
The dream of my return / Horacio Castellanos Moya ;
translated from the Spanish by Katherine Silver.
pages cm — (New Directions paperbook ; 1301)
"Originally published: El sueño del retorno. Barcelona : Tusquets Editores, 2013."
ISBN 978-0-8112-2343-0 (alk. paper)
I. Silver, Katherine, translator. II. Title.
PQ7539.2.C34S8413 2015
863'.64—dc23   2014027200

1   3   5   7   9   8   6   4   2

New Directions Books are published for James Laughlin
by New Directions Publishing Corporation
80 Eighth Avenue, New York 10011

For that which I do I allow not: for what I would, that do I not;
but what I hate, that do I.

— Romans 7:15 (King James Version)

You can't spend your life returning, especially to that cesspool
of a country of yours, that disaster they've turned your parents'
home into, just so you can say hi or bring us words of consolation.
Here, every act of pity is cruel if it doesn't set something on fire.
Every sign of maturity must prove its capacity for destruction.

— Roque Dalton, "The Prodigal Son"

1

IT WAS ONLY AFTER ABSTAINING for five days without any decrease in the pain in my liver that I finally decided to make an appointment with Don Chente Alvarado, a doctor Muñecón had recommended long before but whom I hadn't yet called, still hoping that my favorite doctor would finally answer the many calls I'd made to him all week without anybody picking up, which made me assume that he and his secretary were both on vacation. It was only when a woman answered and told me that this was no longer Dr. Molins's office, that in fact Dr. Molins no longer had an office because he had returned to his native Catalonia two months before—which made the pain in my liver go from bad to worse at the mere thought of being hospitalized—that I immediately called Muñecón to get Don Chente Alvarado's phone number then dialed it to request an urgent appointment.

That afternoon, I made my way to the building where Don Chente lived on San Lorenzo Street in Colonia Del Valle, full of every possible prejudice because I assumed that he was an allopath who would use any pretext to poison me with chemicals and then charge me an arm and a leg for the consultation—according to what Muñecón told me, Don Chente had been one of the doctors most coveted by wealthy Salvadorans before the civil war but had been forced into exile after recklessly treating a wounded man who turned out to be a guerrilla fighter.

I lamented Pico Molins's sudden departure, convinced that I would never find a doctor like him again: a homeopath who had opened my eyes to the scam of conventional medicine and who always saw me as his last patient of the day, when nobody else was there, not even his secretary, so that he could take all the time in the world to listen to my complaints and then change the subject to Mexican politics—about which he loved to speak with scathing disdain—taking advantage of the fact that I was a journalist to milk me for the latest newsroom gossip, all of which I enthusiastically shared with him, stoking his avid curiosity and satisfying his craving to analyze human stupidity. Pico Molins was delightful, and he never charged me for any of my visits, not even the first one, when I came recommended by a colleague who'd informed him of the extent of my penury, the consequence of my forced residence in a foreign country in order to prevent my compatriots from carving me up into little pieces, as they had so many others.

The fact that Don Chente had money to spare was evident from the very first moment the elevator door opened onto a foyer, which was in fact Don Chente's private apartment and meant that the entire floor—the penthouse, I should say—was his, quite impressive given the size of the building and the fact that he was the first Salvadoran refuge I had ever met in Mexico who could afford such a luxury, nor was this just any old luxury, as I saw when a uniformed maid greeted me in said foyer and led me to a small sitting room, where, she said, I should wait for Don Chente. I must have spent about three minutes in that room, scrutinizing the décor and listening to the murmurs of a group of women who were probably drinking tea and playing canasta in a room surely less monastic than the one I found myself in, when a short, swarthy, gray-haired old man appeared, dressed in a guayabera and black pants and wearing tortoiseshell glasses that magnified his eyes; he greeted me with a certain formality, gently and very politely telling me what a pleasure it was to meet me and would I please follow him down a hallway, from which I could not catch even a glimpse of the prattling women, in spite of my curiosity-fueled efforts, that's how big his place was, a hallway similarly decorated in the style of the very wealthy and at the end of which we came to Don Chente's office, or rather, a spacious library that looked nothing at all like any doctor's office I'd ever seen, except for the several framed degrees hanging on the wall behind the desk at which Don Chente sat after inviting me to take a seat.

"How can I help you?" Don Chente asked while I was still looking at the bookshelves and staring at the degrees that certified the man in front of me as a medical doctor, a psychologist, and an acupuncturist, a range of knowledge that made a very positive impression on me, allowing me to cherish the hope that I was in the presence of somebody who would soon afford me relief from my pain. But before I set out to describe my ailments, and perhaps upon noticing my amazement at the number of books on the shelves, Don Chente told me that he no longer officially practiced his profession, he was retired and that's why he didn't have a doctor's office per se, this was his library, where once in a while he saw one or another patient, a friend or a friend of friends, in my case, he was seeing me because of his friendship with Muñecón and his fond memories of my father's family.

"So, tell me …" he said in a gentle, almost timid, voice as he settled into his chair and placed the palms of his hands together in front of his lips, as if he were about to hear a confession.

And then I told him that I'd been having pain precisely here—pressing on my liver—for about a week, that the pain was constant, which made me fear a serious liver disorder, if not something worse, because a decade earlier some cursed amoebas had infested that organ, which was then further weakened by all the poison I ingested to eradicate them, and, moreover, in the last few weeks, I had to confess, I'd been overdoing it with the vodka tonics, anxious as I was about all kinds of problems that were swarming in on me left, right, and center.

"Are your problems that serious?" Don Chente asked, leaning over his desk to pick up a pen and a notebook, then slowly and deliberately beginning to take notes.

At that very moment, before I started to reveal my misfortunes, I remembered my first appointment with Pico Molins about eight years before, when I anxiously described the pain I was having throughout my abdomen, how an ulcer was about to burst, that's what I was complaining about when Pico stood up and looked at my iris, then asked me to stick out my tongue, instead of giving me a thorough physical examination, instead of sending me to have tests done, he simply looked at my iris and my tongue, which, needless to say, made me terribly suspicious, above all when he then proceeded to ask me a series of questions that sounded like some kind of children's game, such as, did I prefer cold or heat, meat or fish, the color red or the color blue—utter nonsense, I thought at the time—and as if that wasn't enough, he then told me he was going to prescribe some sulfur drops, which I would then have to mix with distilled water in a pewter receptacle and take three teaspoons a day—hell, as if drops were what I needed with all that pain ...

"If you like, we can talk afterwards," Don Chente said, standing up and indicating that I should follow him into the room where he would examine me, a small room with an exam table, on which I soon lay down after unbuttoning my shirt and pants—I couldn't hear the murmurs of the tea-drinking women who were playing canasta—and waited for the doctor to pick up his stethoscope to listen to my abdomen, my lungs, check my throat and my reflexes and my blood pressure, all standard practice, not as Pico Molins had done that first time I saw him, when all he did was look at my iris and my tongue, ask me those suspicious questions, give me a medicine bottle with sulfur drops, and tell me that was all, that I didn't owe him anything, without explaining a thing about the ailment afflicting me, and in the face of which I stood without flinching for a few seconds, grateful of course that the consultation had been free but disconcerted by the absence of any explanation about my disease, until I did react, begging him to please tell me the cause of the pain, a normal thing to ask a doctor, but Pico Molins was a little odd, to tell the truth, and all he said was that I suffered from gastritis and colitis due to widespread irritation of the digestive system, and considering the quantity of rum I was drinking at the time and the stress I was under, it was the least I could expect, that I should find a pool and go swimming or some other way to relax if I didn't want to end up with my intestines in shreds.

I felt more confident when I sat down in front of Don Chente's desk after the exam because his behavior so far had been more in keeping with what one expects from a doctor, who first tests the flesh and then engages with the metaphysical, which is precisely what he now did, insisting that I tell him about my current concerns and still not offering any diagnosis for the pain, even though he had taken notes of his findings after pressing my abdomen in a variety of spots; I told him that I was just about to quit my job at a news agency, in fact, I was going to work there for only a few more weeks, my plan being to radically change my life, return to El Salvador to take part in a journalism project I had been invited to join, and which I was very excited about, because the negotiations between the government and the guerrillas were making steady progress, and peace could be glimpsed on the not-too-distant horizon.

"Are you taking your family?" Don Chente asked, leaning back in his chair and pressing his hands together in front of his mouth, his brow somewhat furrowed, which made me think that he considered my decision a mistake. I told him that my wife and young daughter would remain in Mexico, it wasn't as if I wanted to convert my adventure into a tragedy, but once the civil war was over, they would join me. "What does your wife think?" he asked, still with extreme tact and not taking his eyes off me, to which I responded, still staring at the bookshelves, that she had finally accepted the idea, without mentioning that my relationship with my wife had had the stuffing beaten out of it, not because of my trip, but because five years of cohabitation was enough to destroy anybody's nerves, and my departure was to a large extent the result of my need to place enough distance between us to assess whether it was worthwhile to ever light that particular hellfire again.

Then, behaving like an older incarnation of Pico Molins instead of informing me about the condition of my liver, which was causing me so much anxiety, Don Chente started asking me the same childish questions I had had to answer that first time, after which I had walked out of Pico Molins's office—totally incredulous and carrying my little bottle of sulfur drops—onto the main plaza of Coyoacán, telling myself that it had been a waste of time, though fortunately not also of money, to go see a homeopath who had not even examined me, and that I had to immediately find another doctor, an allopathic doctor, which is what I proceeded to do right away, spending a pretty penny on a top specialist, laboratory tests included, so that in the end he could tell me that I suffered from gastritis and colitis due to widespread irritation of the digestive system, exactly what Pico Molins had diagnosed for free after having looked only at my iris and my tongue—what a way to throw away the little bit of money I had!—which is why I decided to take the sulfur drops exactly as he had prescribed rather than the list of expensive medicines the specialist had so solemnly included in his prescriptions.

And the moment I thought that Don Chente had finished asking questions, such as if I liked hot or cold drinks, I took the opportunity to tell him that I had been subjected to the same line of interrogation many years earlier by a homeopath, but that according to the degrees I saw on his wall, he was a medical doctor, an acupuncturist, and a psychologist, but not a homeopath, whereby Don Chente explained that at the age of nearly seventy, he was a student in his last year of homeopathic medicine at the Instituto Politécnico Nacional, the only place that offered such a program, and he thought it a marvelous body of knowledge on a par with all the others he had delved into, a disclosure that made me think this little old man was a true Pandora's box and that he'd probably end up being as good a doctor for me as the disappeared Pico Molins. But I was unable to carry on with my musings because, without giving me a chance to catch my breath and without beating around the bush, Don Chente began a new line of interrogation about my parents, my grandparents, and the circumstances under which I'd spent the first few years of my life, which Pico Molins had not asked me about, as far as I could recall, an interrogation carried out with the utmost tact but one that soon had me telling him that I had spent the first few years of my life with my maternal grandparents, and that my grandmother was a strict woman, to say the least, who loved order and old-school tradition, and that she had raised me those first few years according to that criteria—a woman, moreover, who hated my father more than anything in the world and never ceased to speak scornfully of him even after he'd been murdered. "How old were you then?" Don Chente asked, continuing to take notes. I told him eleven years old, which is why I barely had any memories of him, because he had been killed before the 1972 coup in an incident that remains obscure. "I remember it," Don Chente mumbled, for as Muñecón's friend he had to have known about that crime, which spared me from going into detail—as he put it, he was interested in what had remained in my psychic and emotional memory about my relationship with my father, and not what had appeared in the newspapers.

I am a very anxious person—even though this isn't readily apparent—so I found it intolerable to talk about my family life before Don Chente had revealed to me the cause of the pain in my liver, before he had told me either that the organ was irreparably inflamed and damaged by alcohol and my past illness or that he could prescribe some remedy that would soon cure me. Don Chente met my question with an extended silence, leaned back in his chair, and with a long face that led me to fear the worst, he said, "There's nothing wrong with your liver," an assertion that left me dumbstruck—the pain was right there in that organ—and unable to respond in time to ask him what, in that case, was causing the stabbing pain in my ribs, because before I could do so Don Chente said, "Let me tell you a story that will help you understand." And the old man started telling a story that I didn't pay much attention to at first, so consumed was I by fear, but he soon drew me in, despite his quiet and monotonous voice, and his modest demeanor:

"The different stages mankind has gone through during its millennia of evolution are experienced by each human being over the course of his lifetime on a vastly reduced scale. Before the Ice Age, man, like other mammals, couldn't control his bladder and bowels: he wandered through the mountains emptying them whenever they filled up no matter where he was. The Ice Age led to a great change in civilization. When humans took shelter in caves and were forced to live a sedentary life, they discovered that they did not like to defecate or urinate where they slept, so they learned to control their bladder and bowels and demand that others do the same—which is why the best way to toilet train a puppy is to place his bed where he does his business ... This was also the first time a human being experienced the emotion we now call anxiety, which consists of having to choose between two options: either he satisfies his instinct to empty himself wherever he happens to be, which means he'd have excrement next to his bed, as we call it now, or he controls his bowels and bladder and empties himself elsewhere. In the first two or three years of his life, every human being goes through this entire process that humanity underwent over the course of thousands of years. Do you understand? When a child is being toilet trained, he confronts anxiety for the first time: either he follows his instinct and does his business whenever he feels pressure on his sphincters, or he pleases his parents and controls his bowels and bladder as they've demanded he do. Anxiety and bowel control are closely related. If a child is raised strictly and is thereby strongly repressed, he will have anxiety throughout his life about his bowel control and, hence, his colon. And when, as an adult, he needs to decide between two options, he will feel anxiety, and that anxiety will make him tense up his sphincter and his colon. This is the cause of Irritable Bowel Syndrome, an ailment most human beings suffer from at some point, even if they're not aware of it. This is your ailment."

So captivated was I by Don Chente's story that for a moment I forgot the stabbing pain in my liver, thinking that it had been a long time since anybody had illustrated in such a simple yet profound way a problem that concerns everybody, so captivated that at that very moment I knew this story would go on to become part and parcel of my repertoire of anecdotes, and that at the slightest provocation I would repeat it to whomever wanted to listen, until suddenly I woke up to the fact that it was not my colon but my liver that was hurting, and I said as much to Don Chente and asked him for an explanation. "Your colon is so constricted that it's rubbing up against your liver membrane—that's what's causing the pain," Don Chente explained, then warned me that the best thing for Irritable Bowel Syndrome was not allopathic medicine but rather acupuncture, which treated the nervous system directly, and that if I was willing, he would treat me with needles two days later, to which I answered, yes, yes, of course, though I'd never had acupuncture in my life.

Don Chente stood up, thereby putting an end to the visit, and told me that he would accompany me to the elevator, whereby I hurriedly asked him how much I owed him, my hopes riding high because I'd gotten used to not paying for treatment, so imagine my delight when Don Chente answered that it was nothing, as he'd already explained, he was retired, and if he saw me it was only out of friendship for my uncle, Muñecón, and the affection he felt for my father's family, especially my grandparents Pericles and Haydée, he repeated as we walked down the hallway, where I did not hear the murmurs of the women who surely had finished drinking their tea and playing canasta.

2

I MADE MY WAY to my next appointment with Don Chente Alvarado in a completely different frame of mind than the one I was in the second time I arrived at Pico Molins's office eight years before, at that time ashamed that I had mistrusted his diagnosis and gone to see an expensive specialist, a fact that, to my surprise, Pico Molins discovered only seconds after I had sat down in front of his desk, just by looking at me, and which he mentioned with a certain glee—and not at all as if it had been a betrayal, which is how I interpreted my own behavior—saying that I mustn't worry, people frequently don't trust his little drops, which obviously put me at ease and opened the possibility for us to establish the cordial relationship that ended with his abrupt departure for Catalonia.

"How are you doing? Are you feeling any better?" Don Chente asked point-blank as soon as I came out of the elevator—he was the one who greeted me, not the uniformed maid. So-so, I told him, though the truth was that nothing had changed, the pain was there in my side, and though it might very well be explained by the marvelous story he had told me two days before, the mere fact of being aware that I was about to undergo an acupuncture treatment had made it worse, because if there was anything I feared above all else, ever since childhood, it was needles, and this was my mother's fault, she was the one who'd had the bright idea to learn how to give injections, practicing on my brother and me as if we were guinea pigs, using the excuse that shots of Vitamin B and cod liver oil would make us grow up stronger and healthier, when her true intention had been to amuse herself practicing the aforementioned torture on our aching buttocks every other day for at least three months, I told Don Chente as we made our way down the hallway to his library, without me hearing, on this occasion, any women murmuring, and without me confessing that the prospect of being penetrated by numerous painful needles was keeping me in an exacerbated state of doubt about whether it was worth subjecting myself to acupuncture, or if maybe I should find some medicine that would quickly relax my colon, that was the magnitude of my distress.

"So, tell me, how are your preparations going for your trip? And your relationship with your wife, are things okay?" The old man shot these questions at me as soon as I sat down facing his desk, as if he had antennae that could detect the source of my ills. So-so, I said, adding that we were having some difficult moments, what with my imminent departure, but I refrained from mentioning that she wasn't my wife because we weren't married, a revelation that would have seemed a bagatelle compared to the fact that the relationship had fallen apart two nights before—coincidentally, hours after my first appointment with Don Chente—when Eva, no longer able to bear her guilt, confessed that for the past few weeks she had been carrying on a sexual relationship with a two-bit actor I didn't know and had never heard anything about.

The situation that I refrained from explaining to Don Chente came about in the following way: Eva and I were in bed—she, pretending to sleep, and I, reading a magazine—when I suddenly had an inexplicable sensation, some kind of precise intuition that Eva had something to reveal; so, without taking my eyes off the magazine, I asked her what was going on, assuring her that she could trust me and tell me what was tormenting her, though at no time had she mentioned that she was being tormented nor had I witnessed any such torment; she sat up in bed, arranged the pillows behind her, and started by asking me to forgive her, without saying what I should forgive her for; then she said that she hadn't wanted to hurt me, but she'd gotten carried away like some stupid idiot, and now, consumed by remorse, she was suffering the consequences. "So ...?" I asked her, looking up from the magazine for the first time and seeing that she was on the verge of tears. She told me that two weeks earlier, she had gone to bed a couple of times with an actor named Antolín, someone she had apparently met at her job at the publicity agency, where she was the star of the production department, and they had done it in his apartment, in the early hours of the morning: after dropping Evita off at daycare, she had made her way to this Antolín fellow's apartment, where he was undoubtedly waiting for her very eagerly—I could even picture him naked under his dressing gown, impatient to dig right into Eva's dark and delicious flesh. But, she explained, now shaking with sobs, it had happened only twice— after that she'd felt too guilty and decided she'd never go to bed with that actor again— and would I forgive her and nothing like that would ever happen again. Her revelation was quite a blow to my self-esteem and could have led me to react in several different ways, but I opted for the role of the understanding and affectionate partner who was about to take off anyway and had suddenly happened upon the best justification for his departure, so I took her in my arms, patted her head and told her to calm down—her crying was copious and snotty—assuring her that I understood her, and that her infidelity was proof that our relationship had run its course, been eroded by time and the daily grind. A few moments later, however, I fell victim to a desire for revenge: I had also been unfaithful to her a few months earlier, I told her after we had turned off the bedside light, when a gringa translator named Miriam would come into my office at the news agency, close the frosted-glass door, unzip my pants, and—she, on her knees, and me, keeping my swivel chair from swiveling—suck my member until she had extracted the desired milk, and that she would do this in the late mornings, punctually, like a baby who can't carry on with her day until she's had her bottle, three days in a row until Saturday, when we went to her apartment and discovered that we were a disaster in bed.

None of that, of course, did I reveal to Don Chente Alvarado— I was not seeking marital advice but rather relief from the pain in my side—nor did I tell him about Eva's reaction, when, despite being exhausted from confessing and crying, she turned on her bedside light and sat up, newly inspired to continue the fight, and began upbraiding me for having kept my infidelity a secret for so long, for being such a liar, that her infidelity, compared to mine, was a mere trifle, that's what she said and with indignation, and I responded by saying that this proved that our relationship had no business continuing, she should turn off the light and let me sleep, in a few weeks I wouldn't be there anymore, and she could think whatever she liked—a response that exasperated her even more and made her shout that I was a horrid wretch, completely unfair, a coward who wanted only to run away, this accompanied by a new bout of sobbing that accomplished nothing except waking up Evita and turning my night into a disaster.

"Let's go into the other room," Don Chente said, perhaps aware that the sooner he stuck the needles in the better and that my vague answers about my relationship were evidence of the density of the shit I was not willing to stir up. And we walked down the quiet hallway then entered the room where I lay down on the table after taking off my shoes and socks and unbuttoning my shirt and pants so that my chest and whole abdomen were exposed. "Relax," Don Chente said, because he knew that I was doing the exact opposite, that the closer the moment came when he'd start sticking me with needles, the more I was tensing up in terror, exactly as always happened whenever I was about to get a shot or have blood taken from my arm—my muscles would seize up and make inserting the needle more difficult and more painful, precisely what was happening to me the instant the old man reached the foot of my bed with his needles at the ready; I tried to think about something that would take me far away from the impending torture, so I started to picture in great detail the mornings Eva had spent making love with her two-bit actor, mornings when she would rush into the aforementioned's apartment and immediately start kissing him as he'd put his arms around her and grab her splendid ass; then he'd open his robe so she could lick his chest, moaning with lust, then go down on her knees and take his penis into her mouth. But I couldn't picture anything beyond that because at that very moment Don Chente stuck the first needle between my right big toe and the next one, which was horribly painful and drew from me a cry of protest. "That one's for the liver," the old man said, with what seemed to me like relish, and then he stuck in the next one, and another, and another, until I could no longer distinguish which one was most painful, I never could have imagined anything like this martyrdom, needles sticking out of my limbs, my abdomen, my head, one particularly sinister needle stuck between my eyes, as if precisely in that third eye I had read about in a book by some charlatan when I was a teenager, until finally I felt like I was dying, though the fear was much greater than the pain, I realized as the minutes ticked by, because except for the three needles that really were stinging—including the first one Don Chente had inserted to cleanse my liver—I was getting used to it, and soon my desire to leap off the table like a madman and pull the needles out waned. "Try to relax," Don Chente repeated, "try to feel the nervous energy flowing through your body and especially how it bounces around inside your abdomen, where all your knots of tension are." Then he told me that he would leave me alone while the needles did their job; I listened to his quiet steps as he walked out, the door closing behind him.

"Crazy old fart," I thought, then repented the next moment, just in case the needles would punish me with a renewed and vicious attack for having cursed him. And then I told myself that the only way to control my discomfort was to focus all my attention on the air entering and exiting my lungs, as if I were in a meditation class, my entire mind focused only on the fact that I was breathing in and breathing out; but suddenly I felt a charge from the needle in my calf and my concentration was shattered, and then another from one of the needles he had stuck into my abdomen made me curse the moment I had agreed to undergo such a treatment, but then a few moments later I felt a kind of tingling all through my body that turned into a wholly new sensation, an almost pleasant one, as if I were gaining an awareness of my body that I hadn't had for a very long time. And then I began to fantasize about what I would do when I got to San Salvador, about the exercise regime I would follow to get my abused body back into shape, about the possibility of not drinking for a while so I could devote all my energy to getting the new magazine off the ground, thanks to which

I might realistically hope to find the girl I'd always wanted, but these fantasies didn't last long because then my mind got bogged down in pecuniary concerns, specifically that the director of the agency had promised to do everything possible to make sure I received my final paycheck on time, but I knew all too well about bureaucratic red tape and was afraid that the day of my departure would arrive without my having received my money, which would ruin my plans, or at least my schedule, because without the money I couldn't leave, much less so now that Eva would try to get as big a slice of the pie as possible. And that's as much as I remember because at that point I fell into a deep sleep, for maybe half an hour, until I heard the creak of the door hinges, Don Chente's steps, and his gentle voice asking how I felt, if I had been aware of my nervous energy, and I answered, so-so. "Try to focus all your attention on the spot where you feel the pain," he told me, and then announced that he was going to insert one last needle into my belly, but he said that just as he was inserting it so I felt neither pain nor fear but instead, a few seconds later, I began to clearly perceive the current of nervous energy coursing through my body, just as Don Chente had said I would, and I also perceived a knot in my abdomen where the energy flow was backed up, a kind of roadblock that prevented its circulation: these sensations seemed utterly marvelous to me, incredible, especially when I perceived the exact instant the knot began to loosen and the current of energy suddenly burst through and started to flow. I enjoyed this amazing sensation for a few minutes before I told Don Chente that the knot had come undone and the energy was flowing freely, surely my colon had returned to its natural healthy state and I would no longer have any pain.

With the exhilaration of a person who has, finally, been cured, I returned to Don Chente's library while still tucking my shirt into my pants, wanting only to thank him and get the hell out of there, good health is so precious I didn't want to waste a second of it, but Don Chente invited me to sit down, there were still a few things he wanted to explain to me, the first of which was that although my colon had relaxed, this did not mean that it would stay like that forever, at any moment it could seize up, become irritated, and again form that knot that had troubled me for so long. The second issue, he said, stemmed from the first: only an in-depth treatment that would allow me to shed light on the dark regions of my psyche — that's how he put it — could guarantee a long-term cure, and shedding such a light consisted of bringing to the surface the deepest and murkiest aspects of my relationship with my maternal grandmother and my father, because, according to Don Chente, she had devoted her life to crushing my image of my father with the greatest possible cruelty, and it was precisely this damage to my father figure that was undoubtedly the main cause of my ailments.

"You write poetry, don't you?" Don Chente asked, point-blank, apparently to confirm a rumor he could only have heard from Muñecón. I answered that many years before, I did so frequently, but now journalism was taking up all my energy, and poetry had receded into the background, intolerant as it was to being snubbed. I asked about the relationship between poetry and my ailments, and Don Chente answered that neither of us could possibly know the answer at that moment, but if I agreed to undergo a more in-depth treatment, whatever emerged from it would not only heal my psychic and emotional wounds but also explain and undoubtedly enrich my poetic vocation.

"You refuse to remember almost anything, that's the problem, but the fact that you don't want to remember is eroding your personality from underneath," the old man said, for the first time making an emphatic gesture; I watched him in awe—my thoughts now far away from delight at my cure—wondering how far he would go with this, afraid that the path he had started down would lead to him telling me that I should undergo psychoanalysis, which I would have categorically rejected, seeing as I'd always considered psychoanalysis to be the worst kind of charlatanism, surpassed in its hypocrisy only by Catholic confession, the difference being that the latter is free and the former for rich little boys and girls who don't know what to do with their spare time. But Don Chente's path did not lead there, as I soon discovered, though all his solemn obfuscation made me miss my sessions with Pico Molins, when he and I would deal frankly and effortlessly with all my most difficult crises.

"What I'd like to suggest," Don Chente said, settling into his chair after mentioning the therapeutic virtues of memory, "is that we try hypnosis." This was the last thing I expected—the degrees on his wall certified him as a medical doctor, a psychologist, and an acupuncturist, but now it turned out he was also a hypnotist. "We could try it once a week," he continued in the face of my mute alarm, "starting next Wednesday, if this same time would be good for you." I told him that the problem was that in a month at the very most I would be taking off for San Salvador. "That's fine, you'll see progress after three or four sessions," he insisted. And how could I say no, even though I hadn't yet recovered from my shock, if what we were talking about was a free and novel treatment, one that aroused my curiosity and soon stimulated my imagination, because the idea of being hypnotized made me think that I was about to enter the world of Asian monks and kung fu fighters. I asked him if I needed to prepare myself in any special way for hypnosis, thinking that perhaps he would ask me to go on some kind of diet, as Pico Molins had so that his little

drops would work, but Don Chente told me that no prepara-
tion was necessary, only a readiness to discover things—some
of which would perhaps be unpleasant, that's how he qualified
them—that were buried in my consciousness.

Very strange was my state of mind when I left Don Chente's
apartment after he accompanied me back to the elevator, always
so polite and modest, a manner Muñecón said was like "a wolf in
sheep's clothing," though I then realized it was actually more like
"killing them with kindness," because the old man hid enormous
stores of knowledge behind his somewhat retiring, grandfatherly
demeanor; my state of mind was very strange when I emerged
onto San Lorenzo Street, happy to be pain-free and excited at
the prospect of beginning a process of self-knowledge through
hypnosis, but at the same time I had the sensation that a red light
had gone on far away, I didn't know exactly where or why, a very
small light that did not delay me for even a moment from going
to the phone booth on the corner to call my buddy Félix, who
worked at a magazine with offices just a few blocks away from
Don Chente's apartment and very close to our favorite spot for
sharing news and drinking vodka tonics in the evening, the terrace of La Veiga Restaurant, where we could sit contemplating
the commotion on Insurgentes as well as savoring with our eyes
one or another solid piece of female flesh, and where we would
meet in a half hour to celebrate my cure.

3

THE WEEK BEFORE I once again rang the doorbell on San Lorenzo Street was so disastrous that by the time I was finally standing in front of Don Chente's building I was convinced that this hypnosis session was my only salvation, that things would change for the better after this treatment, and that I might as well tell the old man about my emotional turmoil, especially the tempest my relationship with Eva had become, in the hope that he would give me a helping hand, because the situation, to be honest, had spun out of control, and what had seemed before like a civilized separation had now degenerated into a painful rupture—to say the least—if not a swamp of reproaches, bitterness, and accusations that could only lead to mutual hatred—harmful for both of us and truly malignant for Evita.

Once again it was Don Chente who greeted me as I stepped out of the elevator, and this time the enormous apartment felt empty, silent, dimly lit, as if the old man were its sole inhabitant, a thought that undoubtedly found expression on my face, because right away, as if he'd read my mind, Don Chente told me that he was indeed alone in the apartment, his wife had gone to El Salvador, probably to check their bank accounts, I thought, because Muñecón had told me that Don Chente's wife was extremely wealthy, she was from a family with an unpronounceable Basque surname, Aguirreurreta or something like that, owners of a number of coffee plantations in the western part of the country. "You look a little worse. Has the pain come back?" he asked me even before we'd sat down in the library. No, I answered, fortunately the stabbing pain had not come back—that was all I needed—but I'd been beset by so many troubles all week that I hadn't even remembered the pain, because my relationship with my partner, I told him, had collapsed, not because of my upcoming trip but because of the entrance on stage of a two-bit actor she'd had an affair with, I confessed, and I had the impression that he lifted his eyes slightly, as if to look for the horns on my head, though Don Chente would have been incapable of such a thing, he was much too discreet. He asked me, with as much tact as possible, if Eva had persisted in her lapse, using the word "lapse" as if she had simply taken a misstep and tripped and fallen on her back with her legs spread-eagle so he could penetrate her, hardly what had really happened, with her going off enthusiastically for her early morning fucks, but I refrained from making my accusation too specific and answered only, no, apparently the affair had ended, though when dealing with that kind of sleazy activity it was difficult to know for certain. He asked how I had reacted, perhaps fearing that violence had carried the day, but I told him in no uncertain terms that I had behaved in a more civilized way than usual, having reached the conclusion that we had no future as a couple. "What does she think?" he asked, a look of concern spreading across his face. I told him I still didn't understand her, sometimes she'd assert with conviction that everything was over, but at other times she'd say the opposite, which to my mind meant that she was terribly confused, which had made it impossible for us to hold a calm and reasonable conversation, as was necessary under the circumstances. "Try not to make precipitous decisions; remember there is a young child involved," Don Chente said, picking up his fountain pen to write something down in his notebook.

What I didn't reveal to Don Chente, because I didn't see the point, was that Eva had come home one evening after our last appointment unusually agitated, which made me suspect that she had returned to her adventures with said two-bit actor, so I told her off, sarcastically suggesting that she had traded her libidinous morning escapades for afternoon ones, to which she reacted with a rather disproportional expression of indignation, according to my standards, thereby increasing my suspicions and prompting me to remind her that there was no need to get violent, as far as I was concerned she could do with her ass whatever the hell she wanted and with whomever she wanted. I was afraid this would make her even more belligerent, but the opposite occurred: she went and sat down in the armchair facing the sofa where I was sitting and began to cry, quietly at first and then uncontrollably, so pitifully that I soon cast off my suspicions that she was employing a typical feminine strategy and asked her what was going on, because by now I was a bit alarmed, my intuition having warned me that so much crying could not possibly bode well for me. Sniffling, her hands covering her face, she said: her period was a week late and she was afraid she was pregnant. Flabbergasted, I sat bolt upright, and long seconds passed before I could muster my voice; my insides were being buffeted about by contradictory emotions, and although her sorrowful cries had awoken my compassion, the idea that she was pregnant with the other man's child filled me with so much rage that I thought I was going to explode—I had the urge to kick the hell out of her that very moment—after all, a roll in the hay was one thing and getting pregnant quite another. I asked her if she'd done a test. She said, no, she would the next day, and she explained that she should have gotten her period exactly eight days before, but because of her symptoms she was almost positive—and I understood that "almost" as a final line of defense that not even she believed—she was pregnant. "When was the last time you fucked your actor?" I asked with consummate scorn. She stopped crying, lowered her hands, and looked at me with hatred. "We always used a condom," she mumbled. "So, whose is it?" I asked, my mind stuck on the word *always* that she had uttered so naturally and which led me to infer that those two lewd mornings she had sold me on were nothing but cheap consolation for a poor cuckold and that I'd never know how many times she had actually given herself to that two-bit actor. "What do you mean, whose?!" she shouted, furious, but at that point it really was an act, because as far as I could remember, the times we had fornicated in the last few months had been few and far between—busy as she was frolicking in someone else's bed—and on those few occasions, Eva had assured me that she was not in the fertile part of her cycle. "Idiot!" she snarled, then started sobbing again.

Nor would I tell Don Chente about my via crucis over the following days, when the test came back positive, and thus began the bitter discussion about how to proceed; an abortion seemed to me to be the preferred course of action from every possible point of view, whereas Eva, due to her natural feminine protective instinct, declared somewhat tentatively that she was in favor of keeping the child, though she wavered between that position and mine, constantly bursting out in tears so as to stoke my feelings of guilt, even though she was the only possible guilty party, no matter what, whether the child was mine because she had lied to me about her supposed infertility or, more likely, that due to the excitement and urgency of her initiation into adultery, she'd failed to take the necessary precautions and now the spawn of that circus performer was growing in her belly. But the question of culpability wasn't really the issue, because I was about to leave the country and end my relationship with her, a forceful enough argument in itself against the advisability of any pregnancy, a pregnancy she would have to go through alone and without any support from me, unless she was in cahoots with her two-bit actor, which I asked her about more than once, in which case they might as well leave me out of their soap opera; but Eva stuck to her guns, repeating that there was nothing between her and Antolín, and that the baby was mine, she had no doubt about it, the two times they'd slept together they'd used condoms, and she repeated this with so much conviction that I was on the verge of believing how many times she had lapsed, as Don Chente called it, but not that they'd used a condom, as I told her in no uncertain terms, and for that very reason I'd take no responsibility for the baby and the appropriate course of action was an immediate abortion. By the next day, she'd already made an appointment with a doctor who carried out that kind of extraction clandestinely in a house in Colonia Portales—it was incumbent upon me to go with her because I didn't want to behave like a lout and also because I wanted to be absolutely certain that the fetus would be done away with—a house that, truth be told, nobody could guess was a doctor's office and which I was not allowed to enter—the butcher forbade entry to any third parties, according to Eva—so I waited in the car for a couple of hours, very anxious and with my mind churning a million miles an hour, the situation so tense and anomalous that at first I was afraid there would be neither doctor nor office and that we'd fallen into the clutches of a gang of thieves who would steal our money; then I thought, to calm myself down, that Eva had heard about that doctor through two of her colleagues who had already paid visits to the house that I was now keeping under surveillance. At a certain moment during my wait, I got paranoid that the police would suddenly burst into the house and arrest the doctor and his spread-eagle patients; I watched carefully through the rearview mirror to see if any suspicious characters were hanging around, and I despised living in a country that was so primitive that abortion was against the law, where I couldn't turn to people like Don Chente or Pico Molins to extricate me from this problem. Eva walked out of the house and to the car as if everything were normal, as if she had not just undergone any kind of procedure, which made me fear that they hadn't attended to her, but the moment she got in the car, she collapsed, broke down in horrible sobs—before saying "It's over"—sobs that made me feel as if I'd done something wrong, when by rights we should have been pleased that it had all turned out for the best, which is what I told her, but all she could say was "It was horrible," a statement that proved that she'd inherited from her father, a progressive former priest, a culture of guilt, and that this stood above and beyond her secular education, it was in her genes, I told myself in order to put a little distance between me and the drama, though suddenly I remembered the novel about Evita Peron that I was reading at the time, which claimed that the cancer that killed her had had its origins in a botched abortion.

"It's not surprising that being raised by a domineering mother and grandmother would affect your own couple relationships," Don Chente said, and then asked me to tell him any memories of my father that I did have, even though I'd already told him that I had almost no memories of my progenitor, but I soon found myself talking about my father's passion for fireworks, for lighting firecrackers on Christmas and New Year's, how he would buy bags of rockets, fountains, mortars, whistles, and any other kind of fireworks, which he would then set off with the greatest delight, like a little boy, how he'd spend a good part of those nights with my brother and me and the rest of the neighborhood gang, lighting firecrackers nonstop; he loved them so much that on our birthdays he'd sneak into our room early in the morning while we were still asleep and wake us up with explosions, cheers, laughter, and singing the happy birthday song, *Las mañanitas*. Don Chente listened to me, ensconced in his chair, the palms of his hands joined at his chin, and, even though he periodically leaned over his desk and jotted something down in his notebook, I couldn't tell which details interested him, because I was suddenly remembering about how my father's siesta was sacred, the house converted into a tomb under the midday heat, and my brother and I had to scratch his head, pet his head really, until his loud snores resounded—he didn't smoke sixty cigarettes a day in vain. "Did he ever punish you harshly?" Don Chente asked, in a tone of voice that made me think that I was remembering only stupid things and that nothing essential was coming to mind. I answered that my father had never laid a hand on me, that when he got angry he punished me by making me stay in my room while my friends played in the street or in the backyard, and that it was my mother who shouted and made a fuss, though she dared hit me only once, when I was four years old, and never ran the risk of raising a hand against me again, so great was the fear my grandmother Lena—my protector, whose heir I was—inspired in all of them, I thought, but didn't say to Don Chente, who really didn't need to hear that from me to reach the same conclusion.

What I also didn't tell the old man, and maybe should have, is that the most intense memory I have of my father has nothing to do with his life but with his death, because the night he was shot in the back as he was leaving an Alcoholics Anonymous meeting in Colonia Centroamérica, my brother and I were in bed, and the moment my mother came into our bedroom, a nervous wreck after receiving the phone call, to tell us that Papa had had an "accident" and that she was going to the hospital to be with him, and that we would stay with Fidelita, our trusted maid, and that if they weren't home by morning, which they weren't, we should get up, shower, eat breakfast, and take the bus to school like we did every day ... at that very moment, as I was saying, when my mother came into our room, out of control, I had an intuition that something very important was about to change in my life, that I was about to enter unknown and dangerous territory, an intuition that produced a sensation of fear and helplessness that prevented me from sleeping peacefully that night and stayed with me the following morning, when Father Pedro, the principal of my school, came into my classroom, asked the teacher to excuse me, and instructed me to pack all my binders and books into my knapsack, then started walking by my side, his protective hand on my shoulder as he talked to me about God—I assume, though I was like a zombie so I don't remember his words—until just before we entered the main office, when he told me that my father had died; waiting for me there was my mother's best friend, who stood up to give me a hug, then burst into tears, though she soon pulled herself together and told me that my brother Alfredito would be joining us soon, the principal was going to get him from his classroom, but he mustn't find out yet about our father's death, because he was only seven years old, too young to understand, they would tell him later, after they'd prepared him, whereas I was already a young man, at eleven I should be able to control myself, not say anything or cry while we were in the car on our way to drop Alfredito off at the house of some relatives, who would look after him. And that is what happened: with a knot in my throat, I held back my tears on the way to drop off my brother, and I kept holding back my tears while my mother's friend drove me home, even when we passed the Hospital del Seguro Social, where they'd taken my father after the "accident," as my mother had called it the night before, after receiving the phone call; and I continued to hold back my tears the rest of the morning, at the house, where swirls of people were coming and going, and at the funeral home, where they took me at noon, where I spent the rest of the day and the whole night and the following day, still like a zombie and with a knot in my throat, holding back my tears, even when I went up to the coffin they brought in, and I could see through the little glass window the waxen face of my father, his moustache finally trimmed, and two pieces of cotton wool sticking out of his nostrils, the first dead body I'd ever seen in my life, which completely fascinated me and I went up to stare at several times, holding back my tears, still like a zombie; and when I milled around with relatives and acquaintances, surprised to see the long line of friends from Alcoholics Anonymous who filed sorrowfully past my father's coffin, and still that afternoon when we lined our cars up to drive in a procession to the cemetery; it was then and there, when the gravediggers lowered the coffin then threw the first shovelfuls of dirt on top of it, that the knot in my throat suddenly came undone, and I rushed away from the crowd that had gathered around the gravesite and hid behind an old Kapok tree, where I finally let go of the tears I had been holding on to for so long. And I didn't tell any of this to Don Chente because my whole life, every time I'd wanted to talk about it, the knot would again tighten in my throat, my eyes would again start burning, and I would turn back into a zombie, and now was not the time to make a scene.

"Let's go into the other room," said the doctor. And that's when I became aware of my fear at the imminent prospect of being hypnotized, a fear that took turns in my mind with the idea that the whole thing was a sham, that Don Chente wouldn't be able to hypnotize me, but my fear as well as my incredulity stepped aside to make room for my curiosity about what method the old man would use to try to hypnotize me, which I discovered once I lay down on the exam table, anxious, my eyes glued to the ceiling, awaiting instructions, with that familiar tingly feeling, as if I were about to take my first trip on hallucinogenic mushrooms, which was the first thing that came to mind, that time we climbed the San Salvador volcano to collect the mushrooms that we then put in a jar with honey so they would lose their flavor of dirt and cow shit and that I ate with that same tingling curiosity I felt now, waiting for the psilocybin to kick in, to dismantle my psychic apparatus in order to give me access to new perceptions, surprisingly enough without any extraordinary visions or sounds but rather with a simple opening into a world beyond the senses, where I split off from my self and was able to perceive myself in all my squalor and absurdity, an experience that marked the end of my adolescence and turned out disastrously for one of us, my friend Chino's cousin, who was "left behind," as they used to say, having experienced so much fear at seeing himself as he was that soon thereafter he became an acolyte in a Christian sect.

To my surprise, Don Chente didn't use any newfangled wizardry on me, on the contrary, I had learned the same relaxation technique we now began to practice a dozen years earlier, the technique of focusing all your attention on your toes, then on the soles of your feet, then on your ankles, and likewise along every part of your body, going from your feet to your head and making each part relax through the strength of the mental energy focused on it, which is then experienced as a diaphanous feeling of levity in those relaxed parts. I had done this exercise once or twice alone before falling asleep without attributing much meaning to it, but now Don Chente's voice was guiding me with precision and in a tone I hadn't heard him use before—imperative, profound—a voice that not only indicated which part of my body I should focus on but also wove in sentences that encouraged me to apply more mental energy, so that by the time we reached my head I felt very light, almost as if I were levitating, to tell the truth, and I barely understood Don Chente's whispers because I began to doze off and soon lost consciousness, though deep down, very deep down, there was a constant, indecipherable whispering, like a tiny blinking light in a dark, empty room.

"Wake up!" I heard Don Chente say in a commanding voice. I opened my eyes and saw the same ceiling and then the serene face of the old man behind his tortoiseshell glasses. "Is it over?" I asked as I gained consciousness of where I was and the treatment I had undergone, surprised that the session had been so short, without a single memory of Don Chente asking me anything or of having spoken a word. "That was short, wasn't it? How long was I asleep?" I asked as I got up to put on my loafers. Don Chente looked at his wristwatch and said impassively in his gentle, almost shy, voice: "Just about two hours." Perhaps my bewilderment was greater because I had just emerged from a deep sleep, but when I looked at the time and saw that, indeed, I had been lying there for as long as Don Chente said, though I had no consciousness of anything that had taken place, if, that is, anything had taken place other than a deep sleep, which is what I immediately asked, now truly in the grips of anxiety; Don Chente answered that we had talked a lot, but that I shouldn't worry if I didn't remember anything now, that was normal, later

I would remember what we had talked about—that was the process.

As I was still unable to grasp the notion that we had talked for a long time without a trace of the conversation remaining in my memory, the moment I entered his office again I told Don Chente that I had learned that same physical relaxation technique many years before in San Salvador when I attended several meetings of a so-called Gnostic organization, at its headquarters at 27 Calle Poniente, in Colonia Layco, to be precise. I told Don Chente this to find out if he had known those people who considered themselves esoteric, or if at least he had heard or read something about them. "It's a very old and universal technique," he said and then got quiet before starting to write in his notebook, undoubtedly noting down everything I had revealed to him and didn't remember, which to be honest made me very uncomfortable and tense; I had the urge to grab his notebook and dash out of there, something I'd obviously never have dared to do. I asked if I had told him anything important, but Don Chente merely lifted his hand, as if requesting that I wait a moment, and he continued writing with his elegant fountain pen at a steady rhythm as my anxiety continued to increase, because nobody likes somebody else knowing more about one than one knows about oneself, which was exactly what was happening, though I had no choice but to wait until the old man had finished writing, put his fountain pen back into the pocket of his guayabera, and told me he'd see me next Wednesday at the same time to continue the treatment, that we had made a lot of progress but still needed a couple of sessions before he would be able to tell me anything about it. "You need a lot of patience and trust," he said, standing up to accompany me to the elevator, while I swallowed all my questions, which were actually only one: what had I told him?

4

I THOUGHT ABOUT IT INCESSANTLY, I told myself that it was ridiculous, the events were too fresh, too recent, I wouldn't be able to avoid opening my big trap while I was there, on that table, hypnotized and at the mercy of Don Chente's questions, which is why I should call him the day before and tell him any lie whatsoever to get out of showing up at his apartment, that's what I thought, but Tuesday night came and I still hadn't summoned the courage to call him, as if I were paralyzed and without any willpower of my own, truly bewildered in the wake of the events that had swallowed up both my weekend and my sense of sanity; I had the impression that the fact that I'd been hypnotized was somehow connected to my outrageous behavior, as if the session with Don Chente, the contents of which I didn't remember, had expanded the shadowy realms inside me, realms I hadn't known even existed. That's why, on Wednesday afternoon, my inertia unchecked and in a vulnerable and defenseless state of mind, I arrived punctually at Don Chente's apartment, resigned to the possibility that I would tell him things that would be shameful for me to admit.

The thing is, going crazy happens in a matter of seconds, as I found out that Friday afternoon when I received a phone call from a stranger who didn't utter a word, who only breathed into the mouthpiece for about twenty seconds at the most, long enough for me to suspect that it was that two-bit actor Eva had slept with, and I was about to tell him off, but he hung up before I could, all of which perturbed me even more, needless to say, because that call was proof that Eva was still seeing him, in spite of her protests to the contrary, and also because I suddenly saw myself as the odd man out, the ugly duckling—I didn't even know Antolín's last name much less his telephone number so I could call him back. By the time Eva returned home half an hour later, I had left behind my initial perturbation and was now in an extremely agitated state of mind, because time only makes bad get worse, as I realized on that occasion when I exploded, went berserk, shouted at her that my role in life wasn't to take calls from an imbecile who didn't even have the courage to speak to me, that she was an inveterate liar and had most likely just come from having her pussy pummeled by that two-bit actor, and if she got pregnant again she shouldn't even think of telling me. To my surprise, however, instead of breaking down in tears or becoming hysterical, Eva told me in a consummately detached tone of voice that I should stop acting like a moron, she had not seen Antolín again, but he had taken it into his head to pursue her by telephone, at the office and at home, and she was as put out by it as I was, because that two-bit actor's pursuit of her was affecting her at work; the guy seemed impervious to reason, determined to prove to her that he was suffering because he loved her and was desperate to see her alone, even if it was only one last time, that's how truly screwed up the poor guy was. And it became evident that only the devil himself knows the pathways taken by our self-esteem: instead of feeling pity for the scorned Romeo, I was flooded with hatred and a yearning for vengeance, feelings that were in all respects irrational if what I supposedly wanted was to be rid of Eva, to let her live her own life without interfering in mine, in separate countries and with Evita as the only bond between us; but instead of listening to common sense, which was telling me that she had to clean up her own mess, I started spewing out death threats at the two-bit actor and demanding that Eva give me all and any information she had about my future victim, which she refused to do, obviously, seeing me in such a state of bestiality, she said, a refusal that managed to rile me up even more, until I stomped out of the house, shouting insults and slamming the door behind me. A few hours later I was at La Veiga drinking vodka tonics compulsively, like a fiend, and telling my old and trusted friend, Mr. Rabbit, about Eva's betrayal and how that two-bit actor was pursuing her. "Let's break the sonofabitch's neck," Mr. Rabbit said in a flat voice and without flinching, in that style so typical of him, and he said it as if he could read my thoughts, because the only thing I wanted to do was break that obnoxious Romeo's neck, for even though I'd never killed anybody and lacked the necessary experience to carry out such an act, at that moment I felt elated at the prospect of killing the man who had cuckolded me, my elation increasing by leaps and bounds as Mr. Rabbit displayed so much indignation and willingness to be my accomplice in the execution of Eva's ex-lover; and we aren't talking here about any old accomplice but rather a man who, during his long tenure as a militant revolutionary, had liquidated a number of subjects, and who therefore knew how to pull the trigger without his hand shaking. I immediately gave him all the information I had on the subject and proposed a plan that we set in motion the following day, a plan Mr. Rabbit approved of with keen resolve. When I got home that night, I was transformed, as if I had discovered my mission in life, the one on which I would focus my best resources and all my energy, so I behaved shrewdly toward Eva, conciliatorily, as if the homicidal plans she had written off as mere bluster earlier that evening had been nothing more than that, bluster that wouldn't be repeated, whereby I asked her calmly and with all the virtues of a compassionate man, whether she had persuaded her Romeo to stop harassing her, to which she responded sincerely that she hoped he would now stop calling though she couldn't be one hundred percent sure of it; when we were in bed, I asked her—as if none of it had anything to do with me—if Antolín was at least a good actor, if she had seen the play he was in or had heard anything about it from others, this for the sole purpose of verifying information that would help me carry out my plan the following night. I spent that Saturday in a bizarre, almost jubilant, state of mind, like a naughty child about to get up to some mischief he'd always longed to do, that's what I thought momentarily, even though I had never been a naughty child, and this was something more, something serious, an initiation, as if finally I was going to be capable of carrying out an act that would consolidate my masculinity on many different levels; as if by liquidating the person who had dared offend me in the gravest possible way, I would be fulfilling a manifest destiny that would give me access to a different level of consciousness and personal realization, because from then on I would have a more rigorous understanding of life, a better sense of justice, and I would never forget that everyone must pay what they owe. Mr. Rabbit called me at three in the afternoon, as we agreed, to confirm that we were going to go through with the operation. And at a few minutes before eight o'clock that night, we met in the lobby of the theater behind the National Auditorium but acted like total strangers, each buying his own ticket and entering the hall, where Mr. Rabbit sat a few rows in front of me—he had bought his ticket a few moments before me—which would allow him a better view of the subject, who was also within my field of vision, as I soon confirmed when the play, *La vida es sueño, Life Is a Dream*, began, a boring wordy play that I barely paid any attention to because my eyes were glued to Antolín's expressions and gestures, just as Mr. Rabbit had recommended: that I engage with the subject as much as possible through intense observation, that I even try to get inside his head to see the world as he sees it in order to predict his probable reactions, something impossible to do in a theatrical setting like the one we were in, where Antolín was not Antolín but rather Segismundo, the main character in the play. And while I was observing him in his period costume and listening to him speak in that affected voice, I began to wonder what Eva could possibly have seen in such a specimen, what could have attracted her to him, what had she found in him that I didn't have, questions that began to grate on me and plunged me into a state of odium and a desire for revenge toward someone I was seeing for the first time, someone who had already fucked my woman to his heart's content and in whose face—hooked nose and all—I began to discern the expression of scorn he was reserving just for me, an expression that would turn into terror and entreaty when I began to make him pay for every single paroxysm he had wrung out of Eva. As bad luck would have it, I ran into Carmen, a friend and colleague of Eva's, in the lobby as we were leaving the theater, which made me a little nervous, for although I only said hi to her quickly from a distance, I noticed a look of surprise on her face, as if she already knew about the romance between my wife and that two-bit actor and was wondering what I was doing at his play, as I mentioned to Mr. Rabbit when we met at his pickup truck in a spot in the parking lot where we had a view of the theater's main doors as well as the back exit, because I didn't know if Antolín had a car (the question would have made Eva suspicious); the plan was to tail him all night to learn his every movement, find out where he lived, and thereby decide on the best moment to annihilate him. Not even fifteen minutes had passed since the show had ended when we saw the leading man leave through the main door and walk toward a white Volkswagen bug, which he got into without suspecting that we'd be following him with the discipline and efficacy of an expert in urban guerrilla warfare, which Mr. Rabbit was, and with the hope that he was on his way home to spruce himself up before going out for the night, thereby to discover his lair and assess the option of eliminating him there, though not that night. Tailing him was easy: he drove to the Periférico going south, then got onto Viaducto and took the Avenida Cuauhtémoc exit, which made me think that luck was on our side and our subject was on his way home, seeing that I knew he lived in Colonia Narvarte thanks to Eva's first confession, though she hadn't wanted to name the street for fear that I would act impetuously, nor did I insist, not wanting to arouse suspicion. The whole twenty minutes we tailed him, adrenaline was pumping through my body, I was talking nervously, saying whatever popped into my mind, a bit in a frenzy, to be honest, whereas Mr. Rabbit maintained strict silence, as usual, focusing his attention on the Volkswagen bug until it stopped on Anaxágoras Street and parked, whereas we kept driving by slowly to look for a spot to park a little farther on but with our eyes glued to the rearview mirror, because the worst thing would have been to lose the subject at that moment. "Wait for me here," Mr. Rabbit ordered when he turned off the engine, in a tone of voice I assumed he used for clandestine operations, and, without giving me time to respond, he got out of the car and walked toward the two-bit actor, who at that moment was entering the five-story building where he probably lived. Mr. Rabbit entered behind him and I stayed put, plunged into a state of extreme anxiety, not knowing what to do besides squirm in my seat for a few minutes that seemed to last forever. What would Mr. Rabbit do? Would he simply note the apartment number or would he also enter into contact with the subject? Why had he taken the initiative when I, supposedly, was the one who should have approached the two-bit actor? Soon, I saw my friend returning with slow but steady steps and that impenetrable expression on his face. "Done," he said as he started the car, without me understanding at first exactly what he was talking about, though I assumed he meant he'd found out the subject's apartment number, which is what I told him, but Mr. Rabbit was pokerfaced and withdrawn, not unusual for him, until a few blocks later when we stopped at the first red light and he took the opportunity to take a small pistol out of his jacket pocket and remove the silencer. "It's still warm," he said as he handed me the short tubular device that had muffled the sound of the shot; those fumes of gunpowder were proof that Mr. Rabbit had fired his weapon, I told myself in dismay, suddenly afraid to have the silencer in my hands and throwing it into his lap as if it were burning me. "What the fuck, what have you done!?" I exclaimed, beside myself, because then I fully understood that Mr. Rabbit had just liquidated Antolín. "The plan for today was just to follow him!" I shouted, in shock, truly choking on what had just occurred. "Don't take it personally, but it really was for the best," Mr. Rabbit mumbled, just as calmly, putting the silencer back into his jacket pocket, while I failed to recover from the shock. "Consider it a favor. It's no problem for me to do something like that, I learned how to a long time ago, out of necessity, but you've never done it, and it's better for you not to," he said emphatically, as if thereby putting an end to the subject. And I sat there, speechless, in unfamiliar torment, as if suddenly a huge mass of guilt had slammed into my cerebellum, and instead of the joy that should have swept over me at the death of the person who'd cuckolded me, I experienced a sensation of drowning, suffocation, though it wasn't air I was lacking but something else, because then I realized that it had never been anything but bluster, my true intention had never been to kill said two-bit actor but rather to prove who knows what to myself and Mr. Rabbit about how I could be as brave and resolute as he, about how nobody was going to make a mockery of me without paying with his life, a mockery of the magnitude this Antolín character had made of me could only be paid for with his life, as had now happened without me being able to do anything to fix it. Slunk down in the seat of the pickup next to Mr. Rabbit, who, with a serenity that was diametrically opposed to my all-consuming anguish, was driving toward La Veiga, where we were going to have a couple of drinks to celebrate the "decisive and impeccable" operation, as he defined it while maneuvering the car into a parking place, I understood that deep down I always knew that I would never have had the nerve to kill Antolín, that the whole so-called decision I had boasted about was simply the pretense of a person who knows that at the very last moment he will find the perfect justification to avoid taking action; but Mr. Rabbit's initiative had thrust me into a situation I was not prepared for, because the moment I closed the door to the pickup—still with a modicum of control over myself, even if completely crushed by guilt—I knew that an extremely severe bout of paranoia was enveloping me and that I'd gotten myself into a hell I never thought I'd fall into and hadn't the slightest idea how to get out of. "Don't tell me now that you didn't really want to do it, that you're having regrets," Mr. Rabbit said as we sat down at a table in front of a group of old Spaniards, pachyderms who could be found drinking coffee there at any hour of the day; but uttering a single word would make evident my state of collapse, so I just barely managed to respond with a wave of my hand that meant "it doesn't matter," though at that moment I was becoming terrifyingly aware that the police would not have to dig very deep to find clues that would lead them to me; Eva herself, when she found out what had happened, would undoubtedly point her finger at me, and I wouldn't have an alibi, nor could I accuse Mr. Rabbit, because that person simply didn't exist, he was a clandestine cadre of the Salvadoran guerrillas in Mexico responsible for delicate logistics, someone with false papers, whose address I didn't know, and whom I was able to see only when he contacted me, for I had no means of finding him due to the strict measures of compartmentalization and security he operated under—I didn't even know the license plate number of his pickup truck. "What happened?" I asked in a wispy voice as I waited anxiously for the waitress to bring the vodka tonics. "I caught up with him on the landing. He didn't know what hit him," he said. I tried to imagine the scene—Mr. Rabbit slipping in before the street door closed, the moment he drew his gun, the expression on the face of the person I had known as Segismundo—but I was so agitated that I could not even hold on to these images. "Don't worry, I didn't leave a single clue," he said. The fact that he had wiped off his fingerprints didn't mean that he hadn't left any clues, I told him, my nerves exposed and frayed and I on the verge of losing control, because the plan I had previously deemed well reasoned now seemed idiotic, as was demonstrated by the fact that Eva's officemates would know about her romance with that two-bit actor—women tell one another everything—and Antolín himself had probably bragged to his friends about the great piece of ass he'd had and who'd then left him so abruptly, not to mention Carmen, who'd seen me leave the theater that night. I was completely lost, plunging over a cliff, and my fall would end only with my arrest, imprisonment, and the confession the Mexican police would wring out of me without a savage beating, because I was already broken, an irrepressible urge to confess was already choking me, regret was already gnawing at my chest: I was repentant and ready to be punished. "Calm down," Mr. Rabbit told me when he saw me gulping down my whole vodka tonic in desperation and noticed the queasy expression on my face, as if I were about to keel over. That's when the stern expression on Mr. Rabbit's face relaxed, and I thought I saw a sneer of mockery—now, to top things off, I would become my friend's laughingstock, I thought in a flash of rage, but I deserved all of it, I told myself, now with another pang of remorse. "Nothing happened," he said, smiling, just to try to make me feel better, help me free myself from those tangled webs of guilt, because killing some sonofabitch wasn't such a big deal, that's what he was telling me. And then he laughed, now heartily, and exclaimed, "The guy's safe at home; I didn't do anything to him." But I refused to believe him, he had to be lying to me, otherwise why the smell of gunpowder and the warmth of the silencer, as I pointed out, and the mocking smile that never left his face. "I fired into a flower pot on the landing," he said, now doubled over in laughter at the sight of me so totally perplexed: should I get angry that I'd been the victim of a sinister joke or delight in having had my life handed back to me? "Still want us to break his neck?" he asked, unable to stop laughing.

That's why I said that when I entered Don Chente's apartment to undergo the second hypnosis session I was bewildered and my willpower was quashed, the events of Saturday night having plunged me into a morbid state of disquietude for several days, because without wanting to, I had had to face certain repulsive parts of myself that I refused to accept but whose existence panicked me, giving me the feeling that something very powerful had disintegrated inside me. This time, fortunately, Don Chente led me from the elevator directly to the small room, where I immediately lay down on the exam table, ready to begin the process of relaxation, just as we had done the first time, hoping that as a result of this session I would be able to sort out the muddle inside me, but Don Chente told me to try to relax on my own, to use all my powers of concentration, and he would return in a few minutes, then he left. So I focused my attention on my toes, sending them instructions to relax, without ceasing to think about them for a single instant, until I soon felt the typical tingle of relaxation, then moved to the soles of my feet, then to my ankles, and thereby I ascended along my lower limbs, feeling lighter and lighter, and soon I was nodding off: I was a child wandering through the orange groves on a finca in the Planes de Renderos, a five-year-old child, fully aware of my father's instructions not to pick a single orange even though what I wanted more than anything else was, precisely, to pick one of the oranges I was walking past on that old finca adjacent to the house where we were living, a finca of orange groves where I later came across two people huddled under a tree whose faces looked familiar, but I didn't quite recognize them, two people discreetly enjoying the oranges they had recently and surreptitiously picked and who invited me to join their feast. Then I was awoken by the sound of the door opening and Don Chente entering, though I remained in that state of levity even when he instructed me to open my eyes, which I immediately did, and it took me only a few seconds to recognize the shining object that was moving back and forth in front of my face, it was a silver pocket watch dangling from Don Chente's hand and upon which he asked me to focus my attention, which I did with ease while he talked to me in a way I had seen in some movie or other when the circus magician speaks to a volunteer, who then suddenly begins to follow the magician's instructions without any consciousness of how ridiculous . . .

"Wake up!" Don Chente ordered, but I was returning from so far away that it felt like a lot of time had passed between when I heard his voice and when I opened my eyes; and even once my eyes were open, I remained on the table, not moving, as if waiting to return to full consciousness, in a state so serene I didn't want to leave it for anything in the world. "I'll wait for you in my office," Don Chente said, giving me time alone, for I refused to budge, knowing that the tiniest movement would bring me back, this time fully aware that I might have spent the whole day on that table, that's how far away I felt I'd been—but I soon lifted my arm to look at the time.

When I entered his library, Don Chente was writing down in his notebook what he had extracted from me during the two hours I had been at his mercy, that was how long the session had lasted, I now realized, also realizing that the old man was not going to tell me anything about what I had told him, which didn't really matter to me, unlike the first time, because I was enjoying a harmonious state of levity, of detachment, as if I had been cured of all the anxieties and self-recriminations that had tormented me for the last few days. "You, who are a poet and a journalist, you should take advantage of your facility with words to sit down and write the story of your life," Don Chente told me, lifting his eyes to meet mine. I told him that my life had not been interesting enough to make into a book, though I told myself that my life was in fact interesting enough to make into the very best of books, but there wasn't time, what with my job as a journalist, my wife and daughter—everything was plotting against me. "I don't mean you should write it to get it published, but for yourself, as therapy, to remember and reflect; it would help you enormously," he said before standing up to accompany me to the elevator. And I went outside, where a splendid sun was shining, still enjoying the traces of levity in my soul, thinking that one day I would do as Don Chente said and write the story of my life.

5

I DISCOVERED THAT MEMORY IS UNRELIABLE when I began to digress about how I would start the story of my life if I wrote it down as Don Chente had suggested, a digression I pursued while enjoying a vodka tonic on the terrace of La Veiga the evening after that second time my doctor hypnotized me, a hypnosis session that had left me in a rather peculiar frame of mind, propitious for levity and contemplation. Until then I had been certain that my first childhood memory, the farthest back I could go, the point at which I would have to begin to tell the story of my life, was of the bomb that destroyed the façade of my maternal grandparents' house on Primera Avenida in Comayagüela, a warning bomb detonated at dawn by the colonels who supported the liberal government against which my grandfather and his nationalist cohorts were conspiring. I would have been about three years old at the time, and my memory consists of one precise image: my grandmother Lena carrying me in her arms across the dark courtyard through the whitish dust from the destroyed wall that permeated the air. That was the image I returned to with a certain amount of pride whenever I was called upon to explain how violence had taken root in me at the very beginning of my life, though I would have to add "of my conscious life," because violence takes root at the very first instant of each and every person's life: it's not for nothing that we enter this world crying and making our mothers writhe in pain, I told myself as I took another sip of my vodka tonic and asked myself when my buddy Félix, who'd promised to meet me on the terrace of La Veiga in a half hour at the most, would show up. The truth is, I suddenly found myself wondering, perhaps as a result of my peculiar and persistent mood, how this almost cinematic image had lodged itself in my memory, considering the fact that if I was in my grandmother Lena's arms, it wouldn't have been possible for me to see myself from the outside, to be the person standing in the hallway and watching a woman in her fifties rushing across a dark courtyard carrying a child in her arms, for that was the image that had lodged in my memory; it wouldn't have been possible to be in my grandmother Lena's arms and at the same time in the hallway watching the scene, I told myself with increasing stupefaction, because if I was doubting the veracity of my first memory, how unimaginably difficult it would be to slog through every incident I'd experienced in my life. The only way to confirm what my memory was telling me was to travel to Honduras to ask my grandmother Lena, I thought as I observed the bustle of pedestrians and the tumult of buses and cars on Insurgentes, but I soon thought better of it, it would be utterly senseless to go visit my grandmother Lena, who, at eighty years old, was suffering small strokes that would soon leave her in a state of limbo, and perhaps my memory had been shaped precisely by what she had repeated to me over and over again, whenever her buttons got pressed and she'd begin to rant against the Liberals, whom she never distinguished from the Communists, blaming all of them for whatever was wrong with her country; moreover, I had absolutely no interest in traveling to Honduras for the sole purpose of underpinning my first memory so that I could collect material for an autobiography I would never write—El Salvador was my upcoming destination, I told myself then signaled to the waitress, who had just come out onto the terrace, to bring me another vodka tonic, for I was craving a little more alcohol so I could maintain that peculiar mood Don Chente had left me in.

But my mind had already started down the wrong path: by shaking the foundations of my first memory, I had set in motion the pendulum that was now carrying me at enormous speed from tranquillity to disquietude, because the memory of the bombing was not encapsulated outside of time but rather served as the foundation for important images of myself that were now beginning to falter, like the image of myself as a child who cried with fear every time I heard a siren, whether it was the police or a fire truck or an ambulance, how I would be gripped by dread just hearing the shriek of a siren, precisely as a result of the trauma caused by the aforementioned bombing, for the first thing I must have heard when I crossed the courtyard in my grandmother Lena's arms was the shriek of the sirens as they were approaching, and I can still see myself as a child with my grandparents on a balcony on Comayagüela's Avenida Central watching a parade, perhaps celebrating the coup d'état that allowed my grandfather and his cohorts to finally get rid of the liberal government that had bombed us; when the parade sirens went off, I flew into a panic and began to cry uncontrollably. A traumatized child who broke out in tears of dread at the shriek of a siren: that was me, until who knows how or at what age—I have no memory of the precise moment—I turned into a normal child who could hear the shriek of a siren without crying or getting upset, which is rather unusual if one considers that I achieved this without therapy or any other help, and I have no awareness of having done so, as I said, for I lost my fear without making any particular effort, in the same way one loses one's baby teeth. Then, to my surprise, I discovered that I had no memory of those sirens approaching my grandparents' house immediately after the bombing, the ones that would have caused the aforementioned trauma, no matter how much I closed my eyes on the terrace of La Veiga and attempted to recall the shriek of those sirens that prompted my childhood fear; there was no trace in my auditory memory, only silence, which led me to wonder where I had gotten the idea that my childhood cries were the result of that bombing, if that had been my idea at all, if it wasn't something else that my grandmother Lena had planted in my head and that I had then turned into a memory...

"Are you waiting for your friend?" the waitress asked, taking me by surprise; I had not seen her approach, perhaps because I'd closed my eyes while searching my mind for a memory that didn't exist.

"You startled me," I managed to say, sitting up straighter as she placed the vodka tonic down on the table.

And I told her, yes, my buddy Félix would soon show up, as long as no last-minute problems arose at the magazine, though I immediately asked myself if she had meant Mr. Rabbit, with whom I'd come to this terrace a couple of times. But why should I care whom the waitress had in mind, considering the scale of what had just happened to me: the simple act of attempting to establish my first childhood memory in order to decide where to start telling the story of my life had turned into an unanticipated labor that threatened to foment dangerous internal chaos, which made me suspect that Don Chente's suggestion that I write my autobiography had not been fortuitous—there was a hidden motive behind the old man's suggestion that was somehow related to the hypnosis sessions I had undergone. And to confirm this, I decided to persist in the task of scrounging around in my memory, for under certain conditions obstinacy can be a virtue; I then tried to establish my second memory, which would have come after the bombing—what a great title for the first chapter of an autobiography, if you'll excuse the digression, "After the Bombing," a splendid title, I repeated to myself enthusiastically, as if I were hard at work writing the story of my life. The second event from my childhood that had taken root in my memory occurred at the Montessori nursery school, where I was a distinguished student, a nursery school where one morning one of my classmates had the gall to take my blocks away from me, indeed, with the height of insolence he took my blocks and refused to give them back, despite my pleas, at which point I succumbed to a process of internal combustion and then reacted in an unexpected way, because the only thing that occurred to me to do was pick up in my right hand a wooden block that was still in my possession, and, at a moment when the bully was not paying attention, attack him with all my might, bashing him on the head again and again and again; I bashed that wooden block into the head of said child until his cries of pain caught the attention of our teacher, who quickly bent down and picked me up while other teachers rushed in to help the bully, who was lying on the ground, his head a bloody mess. According to my memory, the bully was taken to the emergency room and they locked me up in the office to wait for my mother, who was an English teacher at the same nursery school, and thanks to her intercession I was not expelled but only received a reprimand of which I have no memory at all, as I also

have none of my little classmate who wanted to steal my blocks
and ended up with his head bashed in, a boy who from that moment on would surely think long and hard before trying to take
something that didn't belong to him; it was at that moment long
ago that I understood that the origin of violence is man's desire
to take what does not belong to him, forgive me the repetition
and the pontificating tone.

Now that I was taking comfort in that second memory, and as
I sipped my vodka tonic on the terrace of La Veiga and contemplated the pedestrians walking quickly along Insurgentes, I told
myself that if they hadn't expelled me from Montessori, if I had
only received a mild reprimand, it was not because my mother
worked there as a teacher but rather because my grandfather
was, at the time, president of the powerful Partido Nacional, but
above all because my grandmother was Doña Lena Mira Brossa,
a woman with a tempestuous character and an explosive temper,
whom the owner and director of the nursery school must have
feared—as was only prudent—for I haven't the slightest doubt
that the instant she found out about the attempted robbery of my
blocks and subsequent bloody developments, my grandmother
Lena had taken my side, blaming my bully of a classmate in the
harshest possible terms for not respecting private property—this
was the mind-set she was famous for—and that she had threatened and berated the teacher in charge of playtime for not having paid due attention, not having stopped the young delinquent
the moment he attempted to seize control of something that belonged to her little prince—that would be me—her only grand-
child at the time. I savored the vodka, pleased that there was no
fissure in this, my second childhood memory, and I also polished
up my self-esteem a little, perhaps even puffing out my chest in
that chair where I was sitting and drinking, because it was obvi-

ous that from a tender age I had been able to react decisively to injustice and take unexpected and devastating action against anyone who tried to take advantage of my apparent vulnerability.

Glancing down the side street past Sanborns, expecting to see Félix on his way, I told myself that the half hour we had agreed upon had already passed, and I wouldn't wait for him any longer than it took me to finish my vodka, it was almost nightfall, and I had no intention of getting drunk on an evening when I much preferred to maintain the lucidity I'd enjoyed since leaving Don Chente's penthouse apartment. And I also told myself that it was enough already, this scrounging around in my memory, such efforts served no purpose other than the concrete one of sitting down to write the story of my life, and the only thing I had so far achieved was to upend my serene state of mind, I'd do better to use my free time to put my affairs in order before I left for El Salvador. Instead, however, perhaps out of nostalgia for the serenity I'd lost, perhaps out of simple mental sloth, I turned my attention outward, let my gaze drift off and alight upon the passersby as I tried to imagine the world that afflicted them from looking at their faces, letting my restless mind play around at will, and from digression to digression I was soon remembering a dream I had had a few days before, really a kind of nightmare, vague in its development but blunt by the end, as a result of which I awoke, needless to say, and that was the only part I remembered, the end, when I killed someone but I couldn't remember whom I'd killed nor the circumstances of the crime, just the sensation of having killed someone but without a specific memory of the act, the anguish produced by the guilt and the fear of having killed somebody without remembering the act or the victim, that was the end of the nightmare, from which I'd abruptly awoken, needless to say, but without experiencing any relief from the aforementioned anxiety; I spent a long time lying in bed, deeply shaken because something inside me was telling me that the dream was not a dream but rather a message from my unconscious, and that I had probably killed someone and now had no memory of it—my psyche had erased the fact, who knows when or how. Remembering that nightmare while drinking my vodka tonic on the terrace of La Veiga upset me again, just as it had upset me every time I'd remembered it; it gave me a kind of vertigo, as if I were at the edge of a black hole whose unknown strength might at any moment viciously suck me in and carry me off to a reality that I could not possibly imagine, the very possibility of which horrified me beyond all reason. It was at that moment, and thanks to a fortuitous association, that I asked myself with astonishment if I had had that nightmare the night after undergoing my first hypnosis session with Don Chente, if that nightmare had been a response to what my doctor had shaken up in my psyche while he had me in a hypnotic trance. Of course! I told myself with a certain amount of joy, sitting bolt upright in my chair and glancing rapidly around me, as if the people at the neighboring tables might have caught wind of my latest discovery; that was how to explain that nightmare: it was my dark side's reaction to Don Chente's efforts to penetrate it while I had no consciousness of him doing so.

I took another sip of vodka, a bit excited because I was beginning to see some amazing consequences of the treatment I was undergoing, and I presumed that that night, after my second hypnosis session, another strange dream awaited me. I leaned back in my chair, contemplating the glass on the table, which contained barely one last sip of vodka, thinking by now that Félix had gotten bogged down with those last-minute complications we journalists always get bogged down with, and probably wouldn't show up, and that if I had any chance of finding any solace on that terrace, it wouldn't be a good idea at all to have another vodka, the proper course of action would be to pay and make my way to the trolley stop. It was at that instant, while I was enjoying the slow passage of time before taking that final sip, carried away by another association my mind had made with no help from my will, that I suddenly felt the impact, or rather, received the blow that pushed me into the black hole I so greatly feared: what if the crime I couldn't remember was the murder of my little nursery school classmate whose head I had bashed in with the little wooden block? What if this was the death that was buried in my memory, the one I had wiped out through who knows what mechanisms and that now, because of the hypnosis sessions, was trying to come out into the open? Oh my God! I almost blacked out. I closed my eyes. It was impossible, I countered, I would have found out somehow, I would have sensed some hint of having committed an act of such magnitude in my childhood, no matter how hard my grandparents, my mother, and the people in her entourage would have tried to hide the fact, no matter how much they manipulated me until I'd erased it from my consciousness, no matter how they'd moved me to another country, some detail would have had to filter through, a glimpse, an insinuation, something, because otherwise it would have been a perfect crime, I told myself, trying to calm down. But the black hole in my mind was already spreading to my chest—the black hole that terrified me and in the face of which I wanted to flee as quickly as possible—so I compulsively downed the last sip of vodka, hoping it would reduce my anxiety, then looked around for the waitress to bring me the check, hoping to shake off that morbid dynamic of self-reproach I had fallen prey to by setting myself in motion, when it was evident that I didn't have the slightest memory of having killed anybody in my life, because I had never committed such a barbaric act, and only a blithering idiot would pay attention to an absurd dream and agonize over it.

Luckily, the waitress was soon standing next to me, check in hand, asking if I was going to wait for my friend in a tone of voice that made me think that she didn't care if I was staying for a while longer but rather if my friend was coming, which in turn gave me the feeling that the waitress was hoping to see Mr. Rabbit—a man graced with a certain elegance whom I'd been drinking with the last time I'd sat at this same table and she'd waited on us—not Félix, who was swarthy and ugly. I answered that unfortunately I had another appointment, and could she please tell my friend, if he showed up, that I had waited until the agreed-upon time, without specifying which of my friends would come looking for me, I was in no mood to play matchmaker when my sole concern was to set myself in motion, get my mind moving in a different direction, and return to my immediate and mundane concerns, especially the issues I still had to resolve with Eva before leaving for my country—I had to stop, once and for all, scrounging around in my early memories, as it had now become crystal clear that this notion of writing the story of one's own life was a bad business, even if Don Chente had recommended it, and it also became clear that memory is unreliable and can put one in rather a tight spot.

6

HOW SURPRISED I WAS that Tuesday afternoon when I returned home and listened to Don Chente's message on the answering machine, a message informing me that he would have to cancel our appointment the following day because unfortunately he had to leave the country for an undetermined amount of time and would get in touch with me upon his return, if I was still in the city, to continue the hypnotherapy that was doing me so much good. There's no question that the cancellation of my appointment completely threw me for a loop, I hadn't expected such a turn of events, and my first reaction was bewilderment: the voice on the answering machine, identifying itself as Dr. Alvarado, did not match the timbre of the voice etched in my memory, a fact that momentarily shocked me but soon made way for anger—I have always taken sudden cancellations as personal insults—though above all for deep frustration, the truth being that my hopes were riding high that after the next hypnosis session, I would be completely cured, freed from the tangled cobwebs contorting my bowels, ready to leave and begin this new stage of my life; now it turned out that I would have to go without finishing the therapy and, even worse, without knowing what I had revealed about myself to Don Chente while I was in those hypnotic trances.

It sounds strange that I hadn't, until that moment, been particularly concerned about what I'd told my doctor while under hypnosis, but this was my first experience lying on the divan of unconscious confessions, and I expected a subsequent consultation, a summation during which Don Chente would repeat back to me, methodically and with consummate wisdom, what had come out of my mouth during those trances, consequent to which he would illuminate those dark areas of my psyche that were irritating my intestines and were responsible for certain kinks in my character. But now that the old man had disappeared without a trace, I began to have concerns about what I might have told him, which he had undoubtedly written down meticulously in his notebook, concerns that were then aggravated by the anguished circumstances I found myself in the previous weekend, when I had no choice but to help Mr. Rabbit deal with an unusual and somewhat dangerous situation. What happened is that my friend called me on Thursday afternoon from a phone booth, as he always did, to tell me, with his typical verbal parsimony, that he urgently needed to see me, which, coming as it did from him, could only plunge me into my darkest fears, send me scurrying to get on the Metro and ride to the station near where Mr. Rabbit would pick me up at five o'clock on the dot, not one minute before or one minute after, for he strictly adhered to the protocols of clandestine life. While we were driving through the city in his pickup, he shared with me the cross he had to bear, which would soon become the cross I would bear: peace negotiations between the government and the guerrillas were progressing rapidly and showing great promise, so military operations had decreased and any moment now would stop altogether along various fronts, a situation that affected the logistical measures carried out by my friend, who was responsible for guaranteeing the safe passage of weapons through Mexico—from the U.S. border to the border with Guatemala; the negotiations were affecting his efforts to such an extent that he had recently received an order to stop a shipment already on its way and park it somewhere until he received further instructions. "So?" I asked as we waited for a green light on Avenida Revolución, and I had a hunch that I'd rather not hear the answer. Mr. Rabbit, without flinching, said that it had occurred to him that maybe we could store the shipment for a few days at my father-in-law's country house in Tlayacapan, a town located about an hour south of Mexico City, where, it was true, the father of my daughter's mother owned a country house that stood empty most of the time, a house Eva, Evita, and I, along with other relatives, sometimes went to on weekends. I told him he was completely crazy, how could he possibly have dreamt up such an outrageous plan—taking a van full of rifles and ammunition to the house of a man who would soon cease to be my father-in-law and where nobody would understand the presence of a load like that—and how the hell was I going to explain to Eva that now that we were in the process of breaking up for good, I'd had the bright idea of hiding a van full of weapons for the guerrillas at her father's house. "It's not a van," Mr. Rabbit said just as he turned off at the Mixcoac crossing, it being that hour of the afternoon when traffic started backing up. "It's a pickup truck, like this one. Nobody would even notice," he explained. Then he added, "And it's not carrying rifles and ammunition." I told him I didn't understand, so what was it carrying, would he please explain and tell me once and for all if this was another really bad joke like the one he'd played on me about Eva's two-bit actor. "They're telescopic sights," Mr. Rabbit said, and he turned his inexpressive face toward me at the exact moment I felt a cramp in my guts that could only presage the return of that horrible colitis I thought I was free of. "Telescopic sights?" I cried out in disbelief. And then he explained that they were special sights for Dragunov rifles used by guerrilla snipers, sights that gave them accurate aim from up to 1,400 yards away, which allowed the snipers to immobilize an enemy column for an entire afternoon, a single sniper placed in a strategic building could hold off an entire company of soldiers for a whole afternoon, like in that Stanley Kubrick movie about Vietnam, remember? *Full Metal Jacket*, Mr. Rabbit pronounced the title with a certain amount of swagger—he'd been a film buff since he was a teenager, and he thought he had a superior accent in English. I told him I hadn't seen that movie and I had no interest whatsoever in talking about movies, but he'd better look elsewhere to stash that pickup with its telescopic sights because there was always a caretaker at my father-in-law's house, a sharp-eyed mestizo named Odilón, who, at the first whiff of anything suspicious would dig through the boxes, and when he found the famous sights he'd immediately turn us in, and the consequences would be dire. "There are no boxes," Mr. Rabbit told me, with a suspicious frown, which immediately made me think that this really was just another joke that he was carrying to a fever pitch, with who knows what dark purpose, so I kept staring at him with a thoroughly disgruntled look on my face so he'd know it was time to cut the crap, but he remained focused on the road and at the intersection with Churubusco he had to make a daring maneuver to turn off toward Coyoacán. "The sights are expertly hidden in the truck's chassis so that not even the best customs' agents would find them," he said in that victorious tone, his way of mocking my lack of discernment.

It didn't take Mr. Rabbit much effort to convince me to carry out the plan that he'd already concocted, replete with a significant amount of detail: on Friday afternoon Eva, Evita, and I would go to the house in Tlayacapan to spend a final weekend together as a family, a kind of agreeable farewell weekend (with sun, fresh air, and a swimming pool) so that Evita, especially, would be left with positive memories of her father now that I was planning to be gone for such a long stretch, my friend said, as if he really cared about the image of her father my daughter would carry around in her head; that same Friday night, Mr. Rabbit would arrive with the pickup packed with telescopic sights, stay over as our guest, share our meals, and lend a touch of lightheartedness to my interactions with Eva, who had a particular fondness for my "weird Salvadoran friend," as she called him. "And if your wife invites other relatives, all the better," Mr. Rabbit said while he explained his plan at a table in a taco place in Coyoacán, as if he knew that Eva and her sisters were afflicted with that tribal disease whereby either everybody or nobody went anywhere. "A family atmosphere is the perfect cover," he pronounced, green salsa dripping out of the taco and through his fingers.

The ease with which I fell into the trap Mr. Rabbit set can be attributed to the guilt or disgrace I'd suffered after that incident with the two-bit actor, but the fact that a mere few hours later Eva fell just as easily into the same trap could only point to something much more pernicious—for me, needless to say, Mr. Rabbit being wholly indifferent to my conjugal drama—something to do with her having hope that a weekend trip could lead to a reconciliation, hope I was determined to parry the very moment it became obvious to me, when Eva expressed her enthusiastic support for the proposal, which I'd sold to her as if it had been my initiative and not that of the person who had, in fact, concocted it, by explaining without beating around the bush that the goal of the trip was to give Evita one last good memory of our family life, and of her father, repeating in this way my friend's words, and for this reason we should avoid any futile arguments or conversations that would strain the atmosphere during our stay in Tlayacapan. Nothing out of the ordinary happened during the two days Eva and her tribe served as cover for Mr. Rabbit's pickup truck sitting inoffensively in the parking area alongside all the other cars, because nobody there would have ever imagined that the vehicle belonging to "Erasmo's Salvadoran friend" was loaded with telescopic sights; a guy as laid back and polite as Mr. Rabbit usually makes a good impression and doesn't appear suspicious, especially not to Eva and her sisters, but also not to their husbands, who were already used to me inviting a friend from my country to spend the weekend at the house from time to time. Nobody would have perceived anything out of the ordinary if they had observed my seemingly relaxed demeanor as I lay next to the pool in my bathing suit under the sun and the palm trees, a vodka tonic in my hand and more often than not chatting amicably with Mr. Rabbit about a variety of topics; but anybody who was paying closer attention would have been surprised by the state of my nerves, for I was terrified that a special police unit was about to burst onto the scene, acting on a tip about the hidden contents of the pickup truck and brutally arresting all of us, though this would be merely the beginning of a nightmare filled with torture sessions and scandalous press coverage. The fear I was keeping so well hidden made me jump every time I heard any vehicle drive past the house, made me see suspicious characters on every dusty street corner in the town, where we wandered around in search of an ice cream parlor on Saturday afternoon with Evita and her cousins, and gave me not a moment's peace while I floated placidly, belly up and eyes closed, in the pool, enjoying the water and the sun while my pernicious fantasy conjured up a scene in which I was swearing to the police that I didn't know anything about Mr. Rabbit's activities, we were old friends, since adolescence, but I'd lost track of him for many years, and I never dreamed he could be involved in such dangerous criminal activities.

But I am lying when I say that nothing out of the ordinary happened those two days when everything, to tell the truth, was out of the ordinary, at least for me, because Mr. Rabbit's everyday life was always out of the ordinary, considering his profession, his nerves tempered in the fire of permanent danger, and his ability to disguise himself and take on different identities, which never ceased to amaze me. That Saturday night, when the two of us were finally alone and on our chaise longues next to the pool under the star-studded sky, drinking our last vodkas of the day after all my in-laws—who believed my friend was a Salvadoran journalist based in San Diego on his way through Mexico—had left, I told him the story of the most intense experience I had ever had at that house four years earlier, an experience that had changed my life and my understanding of reality, if there was such a thing that could be called that, reality, because experience had taught me the contrary, that many realities overlap in the same time and space, which we don't necessarily perceive, realities revealed to me during the peyote trip I took at that country house courtesy of Eva's best friend, Policarpo Unzueta, an ex-poet who once belonged to a tiny group of self-proclaimed Infrarealist provocateurs, and who was now making films and promoting cultural events. As it turned out, Unzueta, which is what he liked to be called—Policarpo, his given name, was so ugly he tried to avoid it—showed up at the house one day with the news that a friend was about to bring him a bunch of peyote heads from the desert, and he asked me if I was interested in taking a hallucinogenic trip; when I answered enthusiastically that I would definitely be interested, he suggested we go to Eva's house in Tlayacapan, the best place to trip, far away from the commotion of the city and surrounded by majestic mountains. That was during a period, I told Mr. Rabbit—sometimes glancing out of the corner of my eye at the pickup loaded with telescopic sights in the driveway— when Eva's pregnancy lent luster to our relationship, when we spent long weekends at that house so that she and the child growing in her womb would be nurtured by the clean air and the peaceful life, so we agreed that Unzueta would arrive on a Friday afternoon and we would take our trip all that night before Eva's tribe showed up the following day. Unzueta, who'd had several experiences with peyote whereas I'd had none, suggested that I abstain from eating meat or processed foods, limiting my diet to fruits and vegetables, because the cleaner the body, the stronger the effects of the peyote, advice that I not only followed to a tee but also with the zeal of a novice preparing for a rite of initiation, because the truth is, that's what it was, a journey of initiation similar to those recounted by Carlos Castaneda in his books about the Yaqui shaman, Don Juan, which I had read with fascination many years before. "So what happened next? How did it go? What did you see?" Mr. Rabbit asked, very curious, because I already knew that he was attracted to certain aspects of the occult and that during his adolescence in El Salvador he had partaken of the same hallucinogenic mushrooms I had feasted on so many times on the slopes of the volcano and at the beach. I told him that at dinnertime Unzueta made tea with some of the dried peyote buttons and that we then sat down in the same place on the patio where we were now sitting, in those same chaises longues, to drink tea while chewing on fresh peyote, one at a time, button by button, that's the process—chew on each button as if it were chewing gum until you extract its deepest essence. Before we started drinking and chewing, Unzueta warned me that I should also cleanse my spirit of any and all bad vibes, especially any negative feelings I had toward him, such feelings could give me a "bad trip," which would cause harm and ruin it for both of us; he said it as if he'd read my mind, because sometimes I was jealous of his relationship with Eva: it was difficult for me to understand how they could be just friends, for I had been educated in a Marist Catholic school, where there weren't any girls, and my only friends who were girls had first been my lovers, a deformation that rendered it almost impossible for me to understand friendship between a man and a woman without there having been sex in there somewhere. I told Mr. Rabbit that while we were drinking tea and chewing on the buttons, Unzueta explained to me that the spirit of the mescaline, which is what the hallucinogenic substance of peyote is called, would take us each on simultaneous trips by working through different plants, one for each of us, the plant with which we each had the most empathy, in my case that avocado tree, which at that time was sick, I told Mr. Rabbit, pointing to a tree that was now healthier; though before that happened, I added, before that avocado tree ushered me into a different reality, but after we had been ingesting peyote for about an hour, I suddenly had a powerful urge to puke, a horrible wave of nausea sweeping over me, the sensation that the vomit was inexorably rising into my pharynx, where I could barely hold it back, and I was frightened because I had read in Castaneda's book that if you vomited, all was lost, and I asked Unzueta what I should do about that disgusting feeling I had in my mouth, and my fellow traveler responded by telling me to chew another button and drink more tea, not to give up, this was the spirit of the mescaline putting me to the test, these were the dues I had to pay; I should just keep chewing, and the vomit would slowly descend, which is what happened about twenty minutes later, when my stomach relaxed, and the avocado tree went into action. It was at that moment in my story, just as I was getting ready to describe in detail the marvels of my trip, the way my psychic apparatus had broken down and allowed me to observe myself as one observes a stranger, when the doorbell rang loudly, a ringing that made us both jump—it was almost ten at night and we weren't expecting anybody. "Who could that be at this time of night?" Eva said from the porch, while I, in a state of panic, looked at Mr. Rabbit and then at the pickup truck loaded with telescopic sights. Odilón, that sharp-eyed mestizo watchman, came out of his bungalow and started toward the gate, which he proceeded without the slightest hesitation to open for the nocturnal visitor, who was none other than Policarpo Unzueta, as if I had conjured him up, which made me shout in delight, "Unzueta!" as I walked jubilantly toward him, as if he were a gift from the gods, for I had been expecting the police. "We're on our way to Cuernavaca, and I thought we'd stop by for a drink if you were here," Unzueta said—unannounced appearances being his style—before he introduced me to his companion, his older brother, Iván, he specified, pointing to the shorter man with similar features who looked like a civil servant or a cop, which immediately put me on my guard; if there's something I can brag about it's how accurately I can detect policemen and informants, which I again proved that night, when Unzueta's brother said that he was a lawyer and worked at the Ministry of Justice, which in other words meant that he was a policeman *and* an informer, a circumstance that wouldn't have mattered much if the aforementioned hadn't suddenly started showing interest in Mr. Rabbit's pickup, according to him precisely the kind of pickup he wanted to buy—whose was it, where had he bought it, how much had he paid for it. Only Mr. Rabbit's coolheadedness prevented me from having a nervous breakdown (I was that alarmed), true coolheadedness that led him to invite Iván to go ahead and check out the truck, turn it on, listen to the engine, without my knowing what my friend thought of the intruder, if he feared as I did that he was the advance guard of a police unit or just a sinister coincidence. Luckily, Eva told them that they shouldn't even think of turning on that monstrosity with its noisy engine and waking up Evita and her cousins, who had given her a hard time going to sleep, and luckily one of my brothers-in-law, the ineffable Pepe Mata, a first-rate sleazebag of a politician, came to check out the new visitors and changed the subject to gossip about the goings-on at the attorney general's office, where Iván the Curious worked.

That's why I say that the anxiety-ridden experience of that weekend—my constant vigilance of that vehicle loaded with telescopic sights—had made me realize how worrisome it was for Don Chente to disappear with all my secrets when I didn't have the slightest idea what I had revealed to him. Though I tried to reassure myself that the old guy didn't seem like some kind of vulgar informant but rather a decent and even wise person, and that at the end of the day the secrets about my life I'd shared with him were not enough to get me incarcerated, at the most they would make me blush in front of anyone who knew them, and surely at first I could deny that any of it had anything to do with me because the charm of hypnosis is that it reveals the dark zones in our psyches that we ourselves don't even know exist, as Don Chente warned me. Just in case, though, I rushed to call Muñecón to ask him what he knew about our doctor's sudden disappearance and complain that he had taken off when I needed him most, and since my plan was to move to San Salvador in one week at the most, it was unlikely that I'd be able to see him again, and my treatment would remain inconclusive.

"Chente is flying right this minute to San Salvador," Muñecón told me over the phone. Damn, I thought, so the old guy beat me to it, without ever mentioning he was planning to go back himself, so much for any trust he had in me. "His mother died," Muñecón added, so I would understand the urgency of Don Chente's departure, and then he invited me over to his apartment later that same night for a drink, an invitation I accepted right away, even though I was still stunned by the news that my doctor was already on his way to San Salvador while I still had to wait a few days for the news agency to pay me before I'd know the exact date of my trip; and stunned also, though a bit less so, by the death of Don Chente's mother or, rather, by the fact that he still had a mother, something I never would have imagined, given his age. Once I hung up on Muñecón, an idea came to me, the idea that not all was lost: I could see my doctor in San Salvador to continue the treatment if, that is, Muñecón would give me his contact information, needless to say, an idea that even excited me, because nothing would be more healing for my spirit than to finish the hypnotherapy at my new destination, where I was hoping to jumpstart my life and set it on a better path.

Before leaving for Muñecón's place, I decided to rest a little, having spent the morning at the administrative offices of the news agency playing the nice guy so they'd hurry up and issue my check; it's exhausting to deal with any bureaucracy, which embitters the spirit and kicks the bottom out of the meaning of life, so a little shut-eye was just the thing to recuperate my energy and allow me to arrive in better shape at Muñecón's apartment, where the sluices were open and the alcohol flowed freely and whoever couldn't keep his balance would fall down and drown, as had happened to me several times. But instead of lying down on the couch in the living room, as I usually did, I went to the queen-size bed in our bedroom—which soon would cease to be ours and would become only Eva's—in the hope of being comfortable enough to go through the process of relaxation I felt like doing at that moment—the same exercise Don Chente used to put me in a trance—whereby I hoped to recharge my batteries and keep my sights trained on my eventual encounter with my doctor in the city from which we had both fled and to which we were both now returning, though for different reasons. Once lying down, I began to focus my attention on my toes, until I felt the characteristic tingling of relaxation, then I continued along the soles of my feet and up to my ankles, and I proceeded with this familiar method as the tingling spread from one part of my body to the next until it reached the muscles in my face, which is when I began to doze off before falling into a deep sleep. Luckily, I woke up before Eva and Evita arrived home and so was able to remain in bed peacefully for a few minutes in that state of extreme calm, reconciled with myself and the world, a state in which I could assess my own thoughts and feelings about the difficulty I had accepting the life I had been given, and in particular I recalled certain things Don Chente had said about my relationship with the father figure in my life, that black hole of sorts into which he surely wanted to shine a light with the hypnosis sessions, making me aware of the fissures so I could go about repairing them; then the calm turned into profound sadness because little by little I became aware of the very deep disdain that dwelled in my heart, not only for my father and my father's family, but also for my mother, and that all this poison had been injected into my entrails by my maternal grandmother, Lena, who had appointed herself sole custodian of my affection and admiration.

7

I WAS IN RATHER A STRANGE FRAME OF MIND when I left for Muñecón's apartment, convinced that my friendship with the man who was expecting me was grounded in our common affinity for drinks and political gossip, and not in the fact that he was my uncle; I had never related to him as my uncle because when I was young enough to learn to relate to someone as an uncle, he didn't visit my house, his relationship with my father, his older brother, having been characterized by conflict; moreover, a few weeks after my father's murder, Muñecón was forced into exile because of his participation in the failed coup d'état of March 1972, so it wasn't till ten years later that I would get to know him, when I ran into him in Mexico City among a small group of journalists who were attending a news conference called by the guerrillas to announce the launch of their military offensive, a conference I was assigned to cover as a reporter, and Muñecón recognized me as we were leaving and suggested we go have a drink at his place. Since then, I had gotten into the habit of visiting him at least once every couple of weeks, to drink the brandy he generously poured and exchange gossip about the ups and downs of the civil war and its political intrigues with him and his buddies, fellow Salvadorans who were always in his living room, mooching brandy and offering loads of bluster.

I walked down Porfirio Díaz to Muñecón's apartment, which was actually just a few blocks away from Don Chente's penthouse, my twofold purpose being to get a telephone number or other contact information for our doctor in San Salvador and to ask Muñecón a few questions about my father, if the conditions were propitious, because I now realized that in the eight years that I had been visiting him, we had almost never been alone, as I explained above, and we were both probably somewhat phobic about discussing family issues, probably for different reasons, I told myself while I was standing in front of the building, not yet venturing to ring the doorbell, because the fact is I hadn't thought about what it was I wanted to know about my father, or if I was only trying to compensate for the appointment Don Chente had canceled so unexpectedly. Iris, Muñecón's current lover and, though this was a minor detail, forty years his junior, came to open the door; she was a nice girl with generous curves and rosy cheeks, and I couldn't understand for the life of me what she was doing with that old relative of mine. In the living room I found my host and his friend, Mario Varela, a Communist apparatchik who did not inspire me with confidence—so much for my luck, on top of which they'd already gotten a head start on the brandy and the conversation—and in whose presence I saw no point in pursuing any topic other than political gossip, nor would I have dreamed of mentioning my father under those circumstances because the Communists despised him, they considered him an informer for the military regime, as I had read in a history book that accused my father of having informed on a clandestine Communist radio station around 1960, a book written by none other than that clever poet Roque Dalton, so clever that he didn't have the foggiest idea that his own comrades were stringing up the rope they'd soon hang him with; and I suspected that this accusation had been the direct cause of the discord that had ruined the relationship between my father and my grandfather, on the one hand, and my father and Muñecón, on the other, a subject I had never brought up with the latter because there had always been a guest like Mario Varela in the living room and because neither one of us wanted to delve into thorny family issues, as I've already mentioned. So I proceeded to pour myself a glass of brandy with mineral water and sit down to listen to the story Muñecón was starting to tell once again, a story I had already heard at least twice before while sitting in that armchair, because with his incipient senility and the systematic massacre of neurons occasioned by his compulsive consumption of alcohol, my uncle ended up repeating the same stories over and over again, unaware that his guests were bored and listened to him only out of the politeness due from those who are mooching his brandy. The oft-told adventure, which Muñecón dramatized as he paced around the living room with glass in hand, consisted of a surreptitious trip he had taken to San Salvador a few months earlier on a mission to serve as a mediator between his old Communist comrades and his old ultra-right-wing friends—if such people could be called "friends"—to promote secret and parallel negotiations to the ones being carried out officially between the government and the guerrilla leadership, a mission whose culmination had been Muñecón's meeting with Major le Chevalier, the psychopathic founder of the death squads and strongman of the party in power, who had evidently seduced my uncle because there was no other way I could understand how meeting with that infamous torturer could have been for him an occasion of pride and boasting.

For one brief moment, I tuned out, as Mr. Rabbit, aficionado of clichés, would have said; in other words, I took a mental leave of absence from the scene in which Muñecón was repeating the story while Iris, Mario Varela, and I were supposedly listening with rapt attention, allowing myself to be distracted by a voice that I had begun to hear more frequently since the first hypnosis session with Don Chente, a voice expressing its discomfort with what had been until then my routine, a voice that at the moment was making fun of me, mocking the ridiculous lie I'd told myself in order to make myself believe that I went to Muñecón's for something other than the free brandy and the opportunity to show off in that vaudeville of political gossip-mongering; also mocking the ridiculousness of my being there, in that living room, feeling somehow special when the truth was, I was no different from my uncle—in spite of my youth, I also wasted my time repeating the choicest gossip about the so-called political situation to whomever would listen; moreover, I was also allowing myself to slip into the morose state of mind that accompanied that voice, a kind of distancing whereby I could contemplate the scene in slow motion, as if I were standing behind myself, with myself included in the picture, which made me not feel fully part of what was going on even though I knew I was part of it.

But I tuned out for only a moment, immediately silencing the voice resounding in my head, which wasn't *my* voice, and leaving that morose state of mind to rejoin the fray of reactions to Muñecón's story, which ended with the moral that the psychotic torturer had shown more courage and daring than the Communists, who had rejected his proposal to hold parallel and secret negotiations, a moral that immediately lit a fire under Mario Varela's passion to defend his comrades and opened the way for an exchange of conflicting opinions—these being the juiciest moments of those get-togethers in my uncle's living room. A second glass of brandy having infused me with a certain intensity of conviction, and determined not to let the opportunity pass me by, I declared that moral goodness and political efficiency are two very different things, a concept certain leftists—who believe that evil and stupidity go hand in hand when sometimes the exact opposite is true—find difficult to understand: "One thing is to be evil, and another, a fool," I pontificated exultantly. My assertion aroused Muñecón's zeal and Mario Varela's anger, inasmuch as the latter assumed I was indirectly calling him a fool, which was not my intention at all, as I proceeded to explain; nonetheless, I sensed that the atmosphere had gotten somewhat murky and was continuing to get more so when my uncle started talking about how nice the torturer had seemed, courtesy of a bottle of Black Label they finished off while the torturer gave Muñecón details of the proposal he should transmit to the Communists, even if they would surely reject it. Mario Varela's face had been contracting into an expression of disgust as our host elaborated on the comedic talents of the psychopath, so I was not surprised when he leapt up and—on his way to the table to pour himself another glass of brandy—blurted out: "Don't you ever forget, Alberto, that those sonsabitches killed Albertico!" Mario Varela's blow, dealt cruelly and forcefully, created an ugly silence in the room, as well as contortions of pain on Muñecón's face and probably in his spirit, because Albertico had been his only son, and he had indeed been arrested, tortured, and assassinated by a National Police death squad in 1980, when Major le Chevalier was the leader of the death squads that operated within the police force. Iris and I turned toward him in alarm, not because we were afraid that

Muñecón would be felled by that well-aimed blow, but because we knew that if we didn't act quickly he would slip into telling the story of Albertico's death, the long and sinuous story about how his son and his son's wife, a lovely Danish girl, were captured, the desperate efforts that were made to have them released, the uncertainty, the growing terror as the days passed, the anonymous call that informed him of their murder, the bloodcurdling trips to dumping sites around the country to try to find their bodies; Iris and I knew that if my uncle started slipping down the slope of telling that story, we'd all be doomed for the rest of the night, forced to listen to him for no less than an hour, because once I had timed him—once out of the maybe fifteen times I'd had the pleasure of being present for that particular show—and it had taken him exactly one hour and seventeen minutes to stage the tragedy without interruptions, because there was no way to interrupt him, considering the intensity of his pain and guilt, his tearful eyes, his heavy breathing, and finally his inconsolable sobs. That's why, before the ugly silence produced by Mario Varela's blow had come to an end, I hurried to ask Muñecón if he'd had any news of Don Chente, if he had a phone number in San Salvador where I could reach him after I arrived, eager as I was to continue the treatments in order to finish once and for all with my irritable bowel problems.

"Chente's in San Salvador?" Mario Varela asked hastily, also apparently eager to change the subject—he did not have the leisure to feel proud of the blow he'd dealt, knowing instead only the wingbeat of furtive guilt, followed by the fear that Muñecón would launch into his tale of woe, which Mario Varela had surely heard even more times than I had, and had even helped construct, I told myself at that moment, because if, as I suspected, the Communist apparatchik had been Albertico's boss at the time of his murder in San Salvador, it was only logical that Muñecón's moving story would have been based on Mario Varela's version, at least in part.

"Doña Rosita died," Muñecón mumbled after another gulp of brandy, still resenting the blow and collapsing onto the sofa. The use of Don Chente's mother's given name gave me reason to believe that my uncle and Mario Varela knew her well, which seemed a fortunate coincidence that would make it possible for me to insist on the subject, thereby moving us resolutely away from the story of Albertico's death and allowing me to obtain more information about my doctor now that I was planning to see him in San Salvador.

"How long have you known Don Chente's family?" I asked Muñecón, hoping he would recover his exuberance, his narrative élan: it was obvious that he had still not recuperated from the upset the memory of Albertico's murder had occasioned, and he needed one last push to return to the present. "Since 1944, at least," Mario Varela piped in as he savored his brandy, during the so-called general strike to oust the dictatorship of Martínez, when the committee of medical students Chente belonged to was leading the struggle, when many of its members, including my doctor, were arrested. The expression on Muñecón's face indicated that he was slowly beginning to recall something, but soon his features relaxed, and then he began to be who he'd been before the blow had been dealt, immediately correcting Mario Varela: it had been two years earlier, in 1942, during one of his parents'—my grandparents'—many changes of abode, when the Aragóns moved in next door to the Alvarados, he said, and they became friends despite the difference in age between Chente and Muñecón— Chente was five years older than Muñecón, and at that stage in one's adolescence, five years is an abyss—establishing a friendship that had lasted till now and that had, in fact, started when they became accomplices in the art of matchmaking, because Chente had fallen in love at first sight with Muñecón's sister, my aunt Pati, an utterly futile passion because she was already engaged to the Costa Rican who would become her husband and with whom she would live in Costa Rica forever. Damn: till that moment I hadn't realized how close my father's family and my doctor's family were, a realization that led me to think that when Don Chente wanted me to remember my relationship with my father, he was maybe playing cat and mouse with me, encouraging me to shed light on aspects of my life he already knew a lot about. It isn't so surprising, then, that I would interrupt my uncle to ask him if my father and my doctor had been good friends at that time, to which Muñecón hastened to respond that, no, at that time my father was already married and living with his first wife and small children in another part of the city, and surely they had met but never gotten to know each other, I mustn't forget that my father was twelve years older than the man who now stood up, his spirits rekindled, ready to tell the story of how he and María Elena, the family servant, had acted as Chente's matchmakers, their objective being to prevent Pati from going to live in Costa Rica, a story that would not succeed in garnering my attention, which was focused instead on the fact that my uncle was getting drunker and drunker and would soon fall into the incoherent state he fell into every night, which would make it impossible for me to extract any information about how to get in touch with my doctor in San Salvador.

"I met him in the Young Communist League," Mario Varela said, wanting to keep talking about my doctor and not Muñecón's matchmaking prowess, without realizing that the sentence he'd just uttered so casually was for me a huge revelation, which enhanced Don Chente's stature in my mind: the old man wasn't only a medical doctor, a psychologist, an acupuncturist, a hypnotist, and a student of homeopathy, he'd also been a Communist—a kind of modern Paracelsus! I told myself excitedly, for a few months earlier I'd read a biography of this enigmatic Renaissance character, who knew about the inner life and also the outer one—and undoubtedly he would cure my bodily as well as my spiritual maladies. I assumed that it was this Communist activism that had led to his capture for having treated a wounded guerrilla fighter in 1980, and then his exile, as Muñecón had told me when I asked for some information about the doctor before putting myself in his hands, but Mario Varela soon disabused me of these notions by saying that Don Chente had been a good cadre in the Young Communist League "until he married that oligarch and deserted," spoken with such scorn that Muñecón himself set aside his matchmaking memories to turn his verbal sputum to the defense of our doctor, perhaps because he perceived an indirect allusion, the glance of a new blow—he himself had also been a member of the party in his youth, then had left and was now a fellow traveler, as they were called. "Chente has always been a man with left-wing sensibilities," my uncle stated categorically and with a frown. "Why did they put him in jail? Who was he treating when they arrested him?" I asked, throwing in my two cents and still not understanding the whole muddle. "Who knows what organization that bastard belonged to, and I bet Chente had no idea, either," Mario Varela said, with even more scorn, as if my doctor, instead of being a fellow traveler, had been some stupid pawn of the non-Communist guerrillas, because at that time there were so many groups with so many acronyms, and the only thing uniting them was the sectarianism they all fought with.

It was at that moment that I told myself it was time to leave—enough brandy was coursing through my bloodstream—and the

most prudent thing for me to do was to call Muñecón the following day, early in the morning when he was in his right mind, to
find out how to get in touch with Don Chente in San Salvador,
because if I kept drinking, it would take an enormous effort for
me to get myself out of that apartment at midnight, and then I'd
suffer one hell of a hangover, a luxury I couldn't afford given the
number of things I still had to deal with before my departure.
That's what I told myself at that particular moment, but the next
moment I was watching Iris sitting quietly on the sofa, listening
to but not participating in the conversation; she had become Muñecón's lover only a few months before—a chubby girl, who was
studying political science and working as a secretary at the Ministry of the Interior and looked more like my uncle's granddaugh-
ter than someone with whom he shared a bed and paroxysms of
pleasure, a girl about twenty years old in love with an old man of
sixty or so. Damn! I exclaimed to myself, trying to find some logical explanation for such madness. Then an idea flashed through
my mind, not as a suspicion but as an absolute conviction: Iris
was an informer for the Mexican intelligence services, hired to
keep an eye on the plots being hatched in Muñecón's apartment,
the meeting place of Communists and one or another ultra-right-
winger. Damn! That's why she looked so fascinated, if maybe a
little dopey, why she didn't miss a word of what either Muñecón
or Mario Varela said, because afterwards she would have to re-
port everything that had happened in this room to her controller,
I told myself as I contemplated the scene with a certain amount
of horror, convinced that my uncle must have been aware of the
situation or at least harbored suspicions, which led me to another
even worse idea, that maybe the whole thing was a setup, and
Muñecón himself reported to the Mexican intelligence services
... It was to chase away this last idea, to put a stop to the para-

noia that was spinning out of control, that I stood up and walked over to the table to pour myself another brandy, totally forgetting my previous decision to initiate my retreat; I poured myself the glass that would push me over a cliff I never would have even approached if, instead of pursuing my fears' circuitous pathways, I had simply taken my leave.

8

I OPENED MY EYES, and for a few seconds I didn't know where I was, having laid myself low with a binge of such magnitude that when I now woke up to it, horrified and in dread, I didn't recognize the ceiling I was looking at nor the piece of furniture I was stretched out on; my mind was a deep dark well from which I was struggling with enormous effort to extract a few basic images, struggling to comprehend that I was lying on the living room sofa and not in the bedroom with Eva, that I had returned so drunk the night before that I had not even managed to get past the living room or climb the stairs to the bedroom where I would have undoubtedly proceeded to wake Eva up to start a row, instead collapsing on the sofa with my clothes and even my shoes still on, snoring like a fiend, my mouth open and drooling. I assumed that's what happened, as it had many times before, but I didn't know anything for sure, my memory was a black hole, as I've already said, and the last thing I remembered was the moment around midnight when I got into a taxi on the corner of Insurgentes and Porfirio Díaz, a block from Muñecón's apartment, but all images from then on had been erased—paying the driver, getting out of the taxi, opening the door to the house, and falling onto said sofa where I was now lying without budging, afraid that even the slightest movement would make my head explode. Jesus, how had I gotten out of the taxi? And my wallet? I brought my hand to the back left pocket of my pants and felt nothing, my leather wallet wasn't there, I said to myself, terrified because the worst thing that could happen to me at that moment was to lose my wallet with my ID and all my credit cards, when all that was left for me to do before taking off for San Salvador was pick up my final paycheck and buy my airplane ticket, so the last straw would have been for the taxi driver to have taken advantage of my intoxication and stolen my wallet. I turned my head very carefully toward the coffee table, where I sometimes put my wallet, but I couldn't make out what was on top of it because the curtains were closed, barely a ray of light was filtering through, and my already disastrous eyesight was suddenly completely blocked by a surge of pain that very nearly split open my skull; I took a deep breath, brought the palms of my hands to my temples to apply pressure and thereby reduce the pain, and told myself that I needed to get up, no matter what the cost, I urgently needed to sit myself up on that sofa in one single movement, because if I did it slowly, the pain would paralyze me. And that's what I did, boom, the good news being that the first thing I saw was my wallet on the coffee table, hurray; the bad news, that I was in worse shape than I'd thought, as was clear from the way my stomach was churning and my sweat was reeking of brandy, and from the sensation I had that my mass of gray matter was about to explode. It was eleven twenty in the morning, damn it, with so many errands to run and me there prostrate and trembling; I hadn't even heard Eva and Evita leave in the morning. With starts and stops and a few long strides, I stumbled into the kitchen to get a glass of water to douse the scorching heat in my esophagus, actually one glass of water after another, then I prepared coffee in the espresso maker and took a bottle of Coca-Cola out of the refrigerator; first of all, I had to get rehydrated, and I could already hear the footfalls of the moral hangover approaching, poised to attack with all its might, because even though I'd forgotten what happened after I'd gotten into the taxi, the events in Muñecón's apartment began to take clear shape in my memory, a shape that without exaggeration could be described as sinister, because the havoc taking place in my body would soon be joined by remorse.

And while I sat at the kitchen table and drank down the quart of cola, waiting for the espresso pot to boil, the dreaded tape began to play in my head, the scene in which I leapt out of my chair and stampeded across Muñecón's living room to the front door, which I swung open and didn't close behind me, because the only thing I cared about was reaching the staircase and flying down it in leaps and bounds, with Mario Varela at my heels in hot pursuit so that he could smash in my face; this was the scene that would play in a loop in my head, over and over again all through the day, each time making me feel ashamed for my starring role and sending spasms of distress coursing through my spirit, distress I would be liberated from only after I called my uncle to apologize, an act of contrition I was not yet in any condition to carry out; I would let minutes, even hours, pass before I faced the consequences of that fateful brandy, which I never should have drunk, because everything started at that moment when I turned with glass in hand and heard Mario Varela say that Don Chente was suspected of having collaborated with the CIA at the end of the '60s and then recount a putative episode on the shores of Lake Ilopango, where my doctor was signaling with lights at midnight to an imperialist agent who'd spent the night on a boat in the lake, all slander without a leg to stand on, the sort so typically used by the Communists against anybody who didn't submit to their plans, and to which I responded with a clever strategy, that is, using flattery as a tactic, asking him—as if I were really fascinated by his story—about the kinds of signals the doctor was making to the CIA agent, what the goal of said signals was, and how they had found out about it, all the time delighting in the Communist's stupidity because he didn't realize that I was seething with rage and had no intention of letting him scheme against my doctor and get away with it. Then I told him, with feigned enthusiasm, that this was undoubtedly at a time when the country's foremost minds were devoting themselves to establishing a Trotskyite party, and perhaps the incident on the lakeshore had been part of this effort rather than a confabulation with the CIA, to which Mario Varela reacted indignantly, as if I had now insulted him personally, shouting that nobody in El Salvador had ever tried to establish a Trotskyite party, that plague had always stayed far from our shores, and who, he asked, had poisoned me with that nonsense, a somewhat disproportionate reaction, to say the least, if we take into account that both young Iris and Muñecón were staring at him, the color drained from their faces, never imagining that I had pulled that out of my bag of tricks in a flash of inspiration, which I was not yet ready to let go of and which led me to say next that of course somebody had, my assertion was well documented in books and magazines, but each time the Trotskyites had tried to get organized, a well-aimed tip-off to the police had aborted their efforts. "You're talking bullshit and defaming the Party," Mario Varela snapped, flying into a rage. "You're a goddamn fucking Trotskyite yourself." Without losing my composure, remaining quiet yet inspired, I explained that this was not the case, that unfortunately I had been rendered incapable of being a Trotskyite due to an episode in my childhood that had marked me for life, and that I would now recount to them: from the age of ten to twelve, my best friend in our neighborhood in San Salvador was a dark-skinned boy named Eduardo, the son of a lawyer who lived next door and had a vicious and untamed boxer, whose name was none other than Trotsky, a dog they had to lock up in the servants' quarters every time Eduardo's friends came over; and I would never forget how I'd stand out in front of the house and call out for Eduardo through the window, and instead of my friend's voice, I would be answered by Trotsky's terrifying barks, behind which I could hear his mother ordering a maid, "Lock up Trotsky, Erasmito's here!" My story worked wonders at relaxing Mario Varela, moving him from rage to bemusement, there he was laughing his head off about something that had not been very funny when I was a child, because, I continued, due to Eduardo's sister's or the maid's carelessness, there were several times when we'd be playing soccer in the street in front of Eduardo's house and said boxer would come tearing out of the house looking to sink his teeth into somebody's flesh, so at the precise moment we'd hear the warning cry, "Trotsky's out!" every single one of us would scramble up the nearest tree to get out of reach of the mad dog. It was because of this childhood experience that I had been rendered incapable for life of being a Trotskyite—as would be evidenced years later, whenever anybody talked about the great Soviet revolutionary leader and I wouldn't be able to stop thinking about the short rabid snout of my neighbor's boxer—I explained to my listeners, because by now all three were laughing at my story, though I wondered if young Iris even knew who Trotsky was, which at that point didn't really matter, because once Mario Varela had lowered his guard, and while I was pouring myself another brandy, I told them that even though I had been rendered incapable of being a Trotskyite, this did not invalidate the fact that El Salvador could use a Trotskyite party to capitalize on the energies of the intellectuals and, above all, to offer an ethical example that the Communists had been incapable of offering. Mario Varela sprang out of his chair and started telling me off, shaking his fat index finger in front of my face, daring me to give him one single instance when the Communists hadn't risen to the demands of the historical moment, as if history and rising had anything to do with each other, I managed to think before his shouting and his accusatory index finger produced a fatal short circuit, blowing my last fuse, which I now rued as I was drinking my Coca-Cola and listening to the bubbling of the espresso maker in the kitchen. Because it was at that moment that I told him that I didn't give a damn if the Communists had risen to the historical moment or not, that I didn't know if history was a dwarf or a giant, but one thing I did know for sure was that the Communists abandoned their own people to the worst possible fates, as had been the case with Albertico, my cousin and the son of Muñecón—who looked at me now in dismay—whom the death squads had captured the very same day they had captured leaders of other revolutionary organizations, all part of the same raid, but only the Communists had been incapable of immediately denouncing Albertico's capture or carrying out violent street protests that would have forced them to release him, whereas the other organizations had done precisely those things and their leaders had been released. "You're accusing me of something, you sonofabitch ..." Mario Varela snapped, as a challenge not a question—we were now standing up, though face-to-face would be just a figure of speech because the guy was at least a head taller and twice as fat as me. "Settle down," my uncle said in a conciliatory tone, perhaps fearing the first blow. "Things were much more complicated than that," he added, patting me on the shoulder and leading me to the armchair where I sat down reluctantly, my nerves already frayed, and then he led Mario Varela to the sofa at the other end of the room, as if this were a ring and we were wrestlers who had just been separated from a clinch. "You've got a bad conscience, don't you, you asshole!" I shouted at Mario Varela in my nastiest voice, my middle finger raised in a challenging gesture, to which he responded with fury, pushing Muñecón aside and hurtling toward my armchair, which I leapt out of, as I already said, rushing to the door that led to the staircase of the building and then out into the street, for although it is true that said Communist was tall and heavy enough to have smashed my face in with one blow, it is also true that I was twenty years younger, and he would have been hard put to catch up with me.

With my steaming cup of coffee in hand, I made my way back to the sofa where I'd spent the night, not understanding which of my psychic mechanisms had gotten me into such a scrape, which had given me nothing but the remorse that was now eating me alive, self-recrimination for having behaved so badly, for having hearkened back to old patterns of behavior that I thought I'd long since left behind, especially after my hypnosis sessions with Don Chente, which I thought had allowed me to achieve a new equilibrium between my emotions and my thoughts; but no, here I was once again, kicking and screaming in the quagmire of a moral hangover, mortified for having accused Mario Varela of facilitating Albertico's murder eleven years earlier—when the truth was I had no precise information about it, only suppositions—and of having blurted that accusation out in front of Albertico's father. Curled up in a fetal position, my hands covering my face, my stomach churning, and my spirit in great distress, I longed to sink into the sofa until I had vanished completely, then return after being transformed into somebody else; I longed for a passageway to open up above me, which I could scramble through and away, but then I managed to shake my head and tell myself, no, it was Mario Varela's fault for defaming my doctor, I had merely reacted to his slanderous accusations, and since I had no other way to hurt him, I used the same recourse he had used to deal that blow against Muñecón, dredging up the case of Albertico. I should take a shower and then call my uncle to apologize and explain the sequence of events, I told myself as I got up and drank down my coffee, feeling more than ready to escape this overwhelming and morose mood and move forward in whatever way possible, but before anything else I had to call the news agency to ask if my final paycheck had been issued, as they'd promised it would be. I struggled to climb the stairs to the bathroom, where another surprise awaited me: a sheet of paper stuck to the mirror over the sink with a piece of chewing gum on which Eva had written in black marker: "If it's inevitable that you keep coming home drunk, at least don't shout so shamelessly. You woke Evita up." Shout shamelessly? I searched for some memory that would put flesh on the bones of my guilty conscience, but all I found was the same black hole, and I stood there for a few seconds in a trance—the sheet of paper in one hand and the green chewing gum in the other—looking at my haggard face in the mirror, trying to stanch the anxiety that was overwhelming me, telling myself that I'd probably shouted from the living room because otherwise Eva's message would have been more detailed; and while I was fingering that green gum like one of those bothersome pieces of snot that are so difficult to get rid of, I remembered that I had put that chewing gum in my mouth while waiting for a taxi at the corner of Insurgentes and Porfirio Díaz, while hatred toward Mario Varela was still seething inside me even as I rejoiced in the fact that the fat old sonofabitch would never be able to catch me. Next, I plopped down on the toilet, the time having finally come for me to empty my bowels and my bladder, which I did for a long time as I stared at the paper Eva had written, reading the text over and over again, preoccupied and not eager to be consumed by remorse for something I had no memory of doing, until I discovered what didn't fit, the reason for the dissonance, and it was the repetition of the syllables "e-vi-ta," once meaning "to avoid" in the word "inevitable," and the other as the diminutive of my daughter's name, a repetition that showed how little care Eva had taken while composing her warning, and also the mood she was in when she wrote it, I said to myself as I crumpled up the sheet and threw it into the wastepaper basket.

I've often wondered why men always want sex when they wake up with a hangover, whereas for women it's just the opposite, the hangover inhibits carnal desire, or at least that's what I've been told by the women I've lived with, and I've often wondered about it, even though Eva claimed that there was no mystery, masculine desire arises from the stimulation of the prostate by alcohol and by the bladder swollen with urine. But that morning I felt so bad standing there under the shower that instead of an erection and the subsequent customary impulse to jerk off, I had only enough energy to lean against the tile wall—almost nodding off, utterly exhausted—and let the hot water cleanse my body, relax it, hoping that at least a little of its warmth would reach my so badly beleaguered spirit; under the lull of the steamy water I began to feel enormous pity for myself, a bout of self-commiseration that bordered on tears, as if the universe had been plotting against me, a sensation of helplessness and vulnerability that made me slide slowly down, my back pressed against the wall, until I was sitting on the floor under the stream of water. And in this position,

I remembered something that hadn't come to mind for a very long time, but after such a night in Muñecón's apartment it was only natural that it would: the memory of the expression on Albertico's face when he answered, "Because I'm an ass," after I asked him why he was returning to San Salvador when the Communist Party had just publically announced that it was joining the armed struggle and going underground, why not just stay in San José, Costa Rica—where we were talking after the New Year's Eve party of 1980—why risk his life returning to San Salvador in the middle of all that slaughter and repression to work openly for the Party when it looked a whole lot like suicide, that's what I asked him, why return under those circumstances, a question that Albertico answered with "Because I'm an ass," without for a moment invoking heroism or the demands of the struggle, with a gesture of resignation that I'd never seen before; he said only, "Because I'm an ass," a fool, an idiot, as if tragedy were his inevitable destiny, as if he already knew that two months later he would be murdered and that it would be a futile murder, just one of the thousands of murders carried out by the military during that period. And his response, which at the time seemed sad and very close to a cliché employed to avoid giving explanations, that cut-and-dried "Because I'm an ass" acquired, after Albertico's murder, a dimension of fatality that would overwhelm me every time I remembered it and that struck me again now as I sat there under the shower, making me realize that I hadn't appreciated in its true dimensions the effect of Albertico's murder on my psyche, having thought that my father's murder and my grandfather's suicide were the only causes of those twisted features my personality sometimes exhibited; the murder of my cousin was there, crouching, without me perceiving how deeply it had penetrated my psyche, and as I stood up under the shower feeling slightly revived, I told myself that I would definitely have shared this discovery with Don Chente if he'd stayed in Mexico City and I'd gone to that afternoon appointment, the appointment he canceled so abruptly and that at that moment I so sorely missed.

I was on my way out of the bathroom when the telephone started ringing with such urgency that I jumped, and my first thought was that it was Eva calling to accuse me of some other outrage or Muñecón calling to upbraid me for the events of the night before, that's why I waited a few seconds, to prepare myself for the worst before picking up the phone; but what was my surprise when I recognized the voice of the secretary at the news agency, calling to tell me that my check was ready and I could come by to pick it up at my convenience. I was so happy I threw the towel into the air, and with it, my remorse and my hangover, life was finally smiling at me, damn right, then I clapped my hands, let out several shouts of joy, and opened the curtains to let in the sun, I would soon be leaving for San Salvador, where I would start a new life, where I would see my doctor again and continue my treatment. It was in this mood, optimistic and elated, that I decided to call Muñecón to apologize for the scene the night before, tell him that I was buying my ticket that very afternoon and would be flying to San Salvador on Sunday, yes, finally the dream of my return would be fulfilled, and for that very reason I needed him to tell me how to get in touch with Don Chente back home. Once I'd concluded my speech, my uncle told me not to worry about the incident with Mario Varela, he had also called early, contrite, to apologize, occupational hazards, Muñecón declared understandingly, and after a brief silence and in a laconic tone of voice, he muttered, "Chente hasn't shown up." What? "He hasn't shown up. They were waiting for him at the airport and nobody knows where he is."

9

I SAT NAKED ON THE EDGE OF THE BED, the towel draped over my lap, distraught, distrait, as if I'd just been punched and hadn't been able to react, incapable of making any mental connections, my mind a blank, in a kind of limbo, perhaps the amount of alcohol still circulating in my bloodstream and the impact of the news of my doctor's disappearance having created a short circuit that shut down my brain, causing in turn a massacre of neurons that plunged me into a cataleptic state for who knows how many minutes— time capriciously stretches out and shrinks back up under such circumstances—until finally the tape in my mind managed to get unstuck, and that's when I began to react, moving from a state of shock to one of extreme anxiety, not only because of what Don Chente might have been suffering at the hands of the military torturers but also because I understood that the same fate awaited me—the moment I landed at Comalapa Airport, I, too, would disappear into the hands of the military, which apparently is what had just happened to my doctor. I fell back onto the bed and stared up at the ceiling, as if in a trance, telling myself that if a prestigious doctor, married to a millionaire and with no truck with militancy or political passions, who had dared to return to his country only because his old mother had died, if he had disappeared into the hands of those military goons, how much more quickly would they pick me up, an unknown, half-starved journalist with friends in the ranks of the guerrilla armies who was returning with the suspicious intention of starting a political magazine. I kept curling up tighter and tighter into a ball until I was in a fetal position, and for the second time that morning I longed to disappear, to vanish into thin air—anxiety combined with a hangover easily skyrockets and turns into terror. Why, until that very moment, had I been so confident that nothing bad would happen to me if I returned before the civil war had ended? Where had I drummed up such naïve, even suicidal enthusiasm that allowed me to disguise the dream of my return not only as a stimulating adventure but also as my first step toward changing my life for the better? What made me think that the Salvadoran military would understand that I was not a guerrilla fighter but rather an independent journalist, that they would simply forget the stacks of articles I had written against them, the military, during my Mexican exile? Once these self-reproaches had rendered me contrite, memories of Albertico began to clobber me relentlessly, because it was all too obvious that eleven years later I was following in my cousin's footsteps—returning to El Salvador to meet a certain death—but I was even stupider than Albertico because Albertico, a Communist militant, had been conscious of the risk he was taking, which is why when I asked him why he was returning in the middle of the carnage, he said, "Because I'm an ass," whereas I was acting like an utter imbecile, even more unconscious and more naïve— how else to explain the excitement I had been flaunting up till that moment. And then I recalled that morning of January 3, 1980—it is so clear in my mind—when a gringo came to visit Albertico in the large living room of the family home in the Escalante neighborhood of San José, Costa Rica—where I was also staying for New Year's, as I already said—a gringo who introduced himself as a journalist working for a newspaper in Philadelphia or Pittsburgh, I don't remember exactly, who interviewed my cousin supposedly for a feature article he was writing about the political violence in El Salvador, a gringo whom I barely glimpsed as I walked down the hallway but whom I immediately suspected of being an informer, a spy, or something even worse, because as I walked by I happened to hear him asking Albertico about his studies in Moscow, a question that could be answered with total honesty there in that Costa Rican city of lambs, but from the perspective of San Salvador, it could lead one directly to torture and death, which is exactly what happened to my cousin. From then on, I never had the least doubt that the interview with that gringo posing as a journalist was decisive in Albertico's murder: with the information that gringo had gotten out of him, CIA butchers decided to target him for execution, but they would wait till he had returned to San Salvador, where they could sic on him those criminals in uniform, which is what they did two months later; from that moment on, I started suspecting all gringo journalists on principle, whatever their sympathies or the little calling cards they hoisted up their flagpoles—anything you revealed to them or confided in them could get you sent straight to the gallows. Still curled up fetus-like on the bed, wallowing in a pigsty of self-reproach, I remembered that my life was so bound up with the murder of my cousin that I had been forced into exile precisely because of that incident: a few days after Albertico had been kidnapped by police commandos, Fidelita, my mother's maid, returned from the grocery story greatly alarmed because of a jeep parked in front of the house with some sinister-looking goons inside, insolently watching our house, which my mother attributed to the fact that my uncle Alberto — Muñecón — was using her car to drive around the country to search for the bodies of Albertico and his wife, because he didn't have a car, having just returned from Costa Rica; Muñecón was using my mother's car to visit the sites where the police and army death squads dumped the bodies of the activists they had kidnapped and tortured. It was the presence of that jeep with those sinister-looking goons in front of my mother's house that made me decide that same afternoon to leave the country, to get the hell out of there; I had absolutely no desire to be a martyr, and, just in case, I spent the night at another relative's house and went from there directly to the bus station at dawn. How could I, eleven years later, have possibly forgotten that traumatic experience and been so eager to return to the place I had left in so much fear? And what seemed even worse: how could I possibly have any illusions about my return, as if this were the first time I'd returned with the dream of "participating in History," for god's sake, when the fact was I'd returned exactly once before, a few days after Albertico, only to end up leaving in a hurry a few months later, as I've just explained?

I made myself even smaller on the bed, curling around myself in that fetal position until I was almost tied in a knot, clutching the corner of the towel with all my might, as if that towel were my last hope for salvation, the rope thrown to a drowning man in the middle of a stormy sea when there are no more life preservers, a large towel made in El Salvador at the Hilasal factory, as it turned out, its tag showing a painting of naïve, or primitive, art, painted in La Palma, a lovely mountain village in the north, a destination for artists and ex-hippies from the '60s, which had been trapped in the theater of war. And in that particular way the mind

has of making capricious associations, I immediately started remembering that the artist who had founded that school of naïve
painting in La Palma had also been a member of Banda del Sol,
a short-lived progressive rock band from the beginning of the
'70s, a band that attained epic status in El Salvador, especially for
its songs "*El planeta de los cerdos*," "The Planet of Pigs," and "*El
Perdedor*," "The Loser," both composed by a guitarist nicknamed
Tamba, after the chimpanzee who costarred with Johnny Weiss-
muller in an old black-and-white movie called *The Killer Ape*—
the famous Tamba, who years later would leave progressive rock
to become Comandante Sebastián, a mythic figure among the
guerrillas, someone who went from rock-and-roll to the armed
struggle with the same sense of adventure and who would die
precisely near La Palma in an ambush about which I had firsthand
information. I sat up on the bed, as if energized by this memory,
though I kept daydreaming, leaning my back against the wall, my
private parts covered with the towel as if at any moment someone might enter the room, because the truth is, in that house you
never knew, several of Eva's relatives lived in the houses next door
to ours and along the same short dead-end street, and it was not
unusual for her mother or one of her sisters to suddenly appear
in the living room or start up the stairs to the bedrooms without
first knocking on the front door. Tamba's story deserved to be
written, I told myself, like so many other stories from the war,
someone really should do it, though not I, I only had information
about the ambush that cost him his life that day in January 1982,
after he participated in the first guerrilla operation of any magnitude in Chalatenango—a devastating attack on the army outpost
in San Fernando, a town located near La Palma, as I said. Soon I
was trying to remember the details of that operation, which I had
written a cable about the same day it took place, because at the

time I was a reporter for a news agency secretly controlled by the guerrilla organization Tamba was fighting for, details that now, nine years later, had grown a bit hazy, though there was one that would always stick in my memory: after several hours of combat, the soldiers and paramilitary forces under siege at the base decided to surrender, as was confirmed in photographs I saw a few days later, photographs that showed a row of about three dozen prisoners face down on the ground, their hands clasped behind their necks, some of them looking right at the camera, frightened, their faces smeared with dirt, whereas the official dispatch released by the guerrilla organization that landed on my desk stated that no prisoners had been taken, that all the enemy combatants had died in battle. What happened to those prisoners? I asked Héctor, who had led the operation, a few months later. "They got malaria," he answered calmly after recounting the battle in detail and pointing out that the raid Tamba would die in a few hours later, after the guerrilla troops had withdrawn in victory, was carried out by the military commander of San Fernando, who had managed to sneak out of the barracks with some of his soldiers during the early stages of the battle and was such a clever bastard that he evened the score by carrying out said ambush, first attacking the scout, or guide, of the guerrilla column, to whose aid Tamba came, crawling through the bushes and into the circle of enemy fire, though as fate would have it, failing to advance any farther before he was shot, a hero's death, like that of hundreds of fighters over the ten years of war, but this was not what impressed me, I was sure of that now; the image of Tamba I most identified with was of the young guerrilla leader sitting to rest after a long day, his FAL across his lap, listening with earphones to music by Pink Floyd or Yes on his Walkman. It was, of course, that image—like a postcard and just as romantic—that impressed me because Tamba had been the two things I never could be: a composer of progressive rock music and a guerrilla, two ideals from my tender youth that he had managed to embody and I hadn't at all, though perhaps fortunately, I reconsidered as I made myself more comfortable on the bed: thanks to the fact that I was not a rock musician turned guerrilla leader, I could now think about this, because if I had been those things, my fate would have been similar to that of the comrade with the nickname of the killer ape.

Again and suddenly, I felt thirsty, because even though the memory of Tamba's story as Héctor had told it to me had managed to extricate me from the distress produced by the memory of that terror, my hangover was still there, pressing in on my temples and constricting my throat, extracting a high price for my binge the night before. I wrapped the towel around my waist and went down to the kitchen to drink some more water and make fried eggs and more coffee, lamenting the fact that there wasn't even one goddamn beer in that fridge and that the Coca-Cola had already gone flat and telling myself that the best thing I could do was eat a good breakfast so as not to collapse in the street, then leave the house without further delay, even if I felt wretched, because my final paycheck was waiting for me at the news agency; right after picking it up, I could slip into the bar in Sanborns, on the corner of Insurgentes and San Antonio, where two Bloody Marys, or rather Bloody Caesars, would put an end to my malaise and, more important, to all those revolting fears that were threatening to paralyze me. And while I was making my eggs and coffee—my salivary glands stimulated by the image of the Bloody Caesar—I told myself that Héctor's life also deserved to be written down, somebody should do it, not I, of course, I knew only what he told me during those two days together in the forest in the mountains of Hidalgo, around the middle of 1982, where we spent two long nights around a campfire, Héctor recounting his war adventures and me fascinated by what I was hearing: anecdotes from his life as a sergeant in the Argentine Navy, as a Montonero guerrilla, then years later as an officer in the Cuban army fighting in the wars of Angola and Ethiopia under the command of General Arnaldo Ochoa—this had been Héctor's trajectory before he ended up in Central America as the leader of the assault troops on the Southern Front in the Sandinista insurrection. Héctor, who looked like a military man through and through, was an unforgettable character of medium height, swarthy and solidly built, with a furrowed brow and a thick mustache, an Argentinian who was too swarthy and too reserved to be Argentinian, a man who left Che in the dust as far as revolutionary adventures are concerned, having fought in war after war, only to end up in El Salvador after being run out of Nicaragua by the Sandinistas immediately after the triumph of that revolution, because while the comandantes were still singing the refrain "*implacables en el combate y generosos en la victoria,*" "implacable in battle and generous in victory," he, on his own initiative, paid a visit to several prisons and expeditiously executed all the officers and noncommissioned officers in the dictator Somoza's defeated National Guard—only by exterminating them immediately could a counterrevolution be prevented, he explained to me on one of those cold nights next to the campfire in the mountains of Hidalgo; the Sandinistas had gained hardly any war experience from their short war, whereas Héctor had already fought in many others, and he knew that those officers and noncommissioned officers would be the transmission belt of a future counterrevolutionary army, which is exactly what happened a few years later.

The stories Héctor told me were legion, I said to myself with a certain nostalgia as I put the fried eggs on a plate and stood waiting in front of the stove for the espresso pot to boil, with nostalgia as well as another strange sensation, as if an idea were trying to percolate into my brain, an idea that was somehow separate from Héctor and the other memories I'd been entertaining, until I finally realized that there was no reason in the world for me to mention anything to Eva about my doctor's disappearance, telling her would only start her ranting yet again against my return, give her more forceful arguments to use in her efforts to ruin my plans; I felt indignant just imagining her tirade, in which she'd accuse me of playing fast and easy not only with my own life but with the future of our daughter, whom I wanted to turn into an orphan, abandoned and without a single memory of her father. I poured the coffee and tried to calm myself down: eating breakfast under the influence of negative emotions interferes with digestion, and it wouldn't be difficult, after all, to keep the news of Don Chente's disappearance from Eva, because she almost never had any contact with Muñecón, she couldn't tolerate that retinue of drunkards and blowhards that gathered around my uncle; in any case, it would be ill-advised to mention it to her, or to anybody else, I thought again, until I had more information about what had actually happened to my doctor. Luckily the yolks of my eggs were soft and runny enough to soak up with pieces of bread, just how I liked them, not hard and overcooked as Eva preferred, even in this we were incompatible, I told myself as I sipped the coffee and tried to remember those two nights in the forest in the mountains of Hidalgo, where Héctor, warmed by the campfire, confided to me a terrible story: on the eve of that military operation on the heels of which Tamba would die in an ambush, while the guerrilla band, on its way to its objective, was resting next to a ford in the Motochico River, Héctor received word in a coded message broadcast over the radio—as occurs in every

103

war—that his wife had been captured at a checkpoint an hour earlier, a checkpoint on the highway leading to Chalatenango near the El Limón bridge, along the same river they were resting next to at that moment. Héctor's wife was a Mexican named Juanita, a teacher by profession, who was riding the bus to the regional capital in Chalatenango, where she'd be met and taken to the guerrilla camp, a plan that was aborted when the military stopped the bus on the bridge, unloaded the passengers to check their IDs, then took said woman into captivity. Héctor was then faced with one of the biggest dilemmas of his life, a devastating predicament, he told me while we watched the leaping shadows and listened to the crackling of the dry branches being consumed by the fire, because he knew that it was possible for his guerrilla band to quickly traverse those approximately three miles separating them from the government roadblock and attempt to rescue his wife, which would of course have meant scrapping the operation he had been assigned—to attack the military outpost in San Fernando—which in the end he carried out.

And while I was pouring ketchup on the whites of my eggs, deeply moved by the memory of Héctor's story, I came to the verge of shedding tears—it's a well-known fact that we wear our feelings on our sleeve when we're hungover—imagining what it must have been like for that warrior to have to choose between making an attempt to rescue his wife and carrying out his assigned mission, a mission that would be crucial to the progress of the war—the conflict between a lover's passion and a warrior's discipline, a true Greek tragedy, I thought as I sipped my coffee, because in the end Juanita disappeared forever, the soldiers tortured her until she was dead and then got rid of her body who knows how. What would I have done in that situation? How would I have behaved? Would I have set off with my troops to free Eva or persevered in my assigned mission and then learned to live with the guilt, as Héctor had done? But that's all nonsense, I thought all of a sudden, emerging from my daydreams, it's easy to identify with someone else in order to indulge in self-pity, but all it takes is a split second of lucidity to realize the ridiculous nature of one's afflictions: *my* plan was to end my relationship with Eva, that's why I was leaving. And I would never be in a situation like the one Héctor had faced because I wasn't a guerrilla fighter and never would be, given my antipathy to following orders, my total aversion to the demands of life as a combatant, especially the discomfort of carrying a backpack from camp to camp and shitting in the open air, none of which suited me at all—I found that out when I made a futile attempt to be a boy scout and it was confirmed once again during those two days I spent with my Argentinian comrade.

I carried my dirty dishes to the sink, told myself that enough was enough with the memories, it would be best to simply forget what Héctor had told me, as well as what he had taught me, during those two days we spent in fatigues in the forest in the mountains of Hidalgo, where we had gone from Mexico City, where the Argentinian went to recover from a gastric ulcer that had forced him to leave the front, and where he remained for several weeks while being treated for his ulcer— caused by the tensions of war and also, I think, by the repressed torment of having abandoned Juanita—a tumultuous period of repose for the guerrilla fighter, after which he'd return to the battlefield, where he'd die a few months later, blown to pieces by an enemy grenade that fell into the trench where he'd taken shelter during a battle in the foothills of the Guazapa Volcano. I really should change the tape playing in my head, I kept telling myself, because if I didn't, I'd run the risk of another panic attack, especially if I started wondering what I knew that the military might be interested in, what information they would try to extract from me after they captured me upon my arrival at the Comalapa Airport, a panic attack I could prevent only if at that very moment I started to move toward the stairs, knowing that the intelligent thing to do was get dressed and go pick up my check before anything else could happen.

10

TO BUY THE TICKET or not to buy the ticket, that was the question I kept asking myself again and again while sitting on the bar stool and fidgeting, as if there were ants in my pants, having almost finished my first Bloody Caesar and firmly intending to order another, for although my physical discomfort had decreased, the same could not be said of my anxiety, mostly because I had called Muñecón several times to ask if he'd heard any news of Don Chente, two hours having already passed since he announced to me that Don Chente's relatives had been waiting for him in vain at Comalapa Airport; but nobody was picking up at Muñecón's apartment, which made me fear the worst—rather than consider that he had simply gone out to run an errand, as under any other circumstances I would have—and suspect that bad news about my doctor had forced him to go out in the middle of the day, when my uncle customarily stayed put at home.

To buy the ticket or not to buy the ticket, I repeated to myself over and over again while compulsively chucking peanuts into my mouth, the check I had picked up at the news agency burning a hole through my shirt pocket over my heart, waiting for me to deposit it in the bank, something I should have done before slipping into the bar in Sanborns, where I now was, but my thirst was stronger than my common sense, and the moment I said goodbye to Charlie Face, the director of the agency, a Chilean who was much too well behaved to understand the urgency of a hangover, I dashed headlong to the Bloody Caesar I was now drinking, though not without first stopping at a phone booth to call Muñecón, as I already said, without anybody answering as I'd hoped. And my dilemma was the following: to buy the ticket without knowing for sure if Don Chente had been captured was idiotic, but to delay meant running the risk of losing the reservation and of the price going up, as the girl at the travel agency warned me.

The next time I called Muñecón it was from the phone located at the entrance to the restrooms in Sanborns, after I had downed half the Bloody Caesar in one gulp; not finding him and knowing that it's much too disconcerting to be all alone with one's anxiety, I decided to call my buddy Félix, who fortunately was still at the office and also longing for a drink to cure his own hangover, because the night before he had been out partying and had gotten even more sauced than I had, according to what he told me. That's why I was sitting on the stool and fidgeting as if I had ants in my pants, I repeat, because now along with my anxiety about Don Chente's possible capture and disappearance was added another anxiety: Félix had long distinguished himself for his total lack of punctuality, and he was capable of arriving more than an hour late and acting as if nothing whatsoever was wrong. To make matters worse, I was the first customer of the day, and the bartender was busy getting the bottles and other ingredients ready, so after making my Bloody Caesar almost resentfully, he carried on with his preparations without paying any attention to my attempts to strike up a conversation.

That was when I realized that I suffered from a horrifying lack of control over my emotions, as if the serene state of mind brought about by the sessions of acupuncture and hypnosis had disappeared along with my doctor, along with all the positive energy that had suffused me at the prospect of returning to my native country, if you'll excuse the expression, for although I was not born in El Salvador, it was as if my umbilical cord were attached to that place, so young was I when they took me there. I was utterly baffled—my eyes staring at the row of bottles—trying to figure out why and to what extent I had tied my emotional and psychic well-being to Don Chente: how was it possible that after a mere half-dozen appointments I had become so dependent on a doctor? What had I revealed to him? What secret part of my being had passed into his hands so that today I felt so lost at his disappearance? The bartender asked me if I wanted another Bloody Caesar. I indicated I did with a nod; I didn't feel like talking anymore, distraction was the last thing I needed at that moment, because I felt as if a revelation was on the verge of rising out of the depths of my being, as if something dark and mysterious was making its way into my consciousness. And then, for a single instant, I perceived it with extreme clarity and in dismay, but then I immediately shook my head, wanting that memory not to be there but rather to return at once to the dark depths from which it never should have risen. I observed the bartender agitating the metal cocktail shaker and greeting two customers on their way to a table, and I also turned to greet them, as if they were old friends, knowing this was the only way to get out of myself, keep myself at a certain remove from a memory that I didn't want to remember for anything in the world, and that I had never told anybody in my life, one that had now risen from the substratum, perhaps as a result of the anxiety I was experiencing at this crucial moment in my life or maybe because of how vulnerable the hangover had made me, which were one and the same thing when all was said and done, because the image of the Volkswagen bug riddled with machine-gun fire had already penetrated my conscious mind, exactly as I had seen it that horrible morning so many years before in the newspaper column, "Last Night's News," a photo with a caption I read in total shock that stated that the driver of the bug, Gordo Porky, had been shot sixty-four times before collapsing over the steering wheel after a Hollywood-style car chase through Colonia Layco: shaken to the core, I suffered a kind of breakdown at that moment, which could only be expected because Gordo Porky had driven me home in that very same bug just two hours before they ambushed him; we had stayed at the law school cafeteria, drinking beer and chatting, as we did fairly often after the language theory class we were taking together. And stuck to the image of Gordo Porky, as if to the other side of a coin, was a sinister scene, and now here it appeared again, right in the bar in Sanborns, against my will and dripping like sulfuric acid into my conscience: a few days before the ambush, I met two professors in a classroom in the Philosophy Department, two professors we later found out were informants for the army intelligence services and who wanted to talk to me about something academic, but the truth was they were conducting a kind of casual interrogation, during which they brought up, as if in passing, the adventures of Gordo Porky and me, the naïve one with the big mouth … Shit! I exclaimed to myself, and the word might even have formed on my lips, because I slapped the palm of my hand against my forehead, like someone who'd suddenly discovered he'd misplaced the winning ticket of the big lottery prize—even the waiter coming toward me with my Bloody Caesar thought it best to ask me if I was okay. "No, it's nothing, I just forgot something at the office," I managed to mumble, just to get rid of him, then immediately raised the glass as if to offer a toast, trying to control the grimace of panic that was on the verge of disfiguring my face, because now I knew what I had revealed to Don Chente and that could surely be found in his notebook. I already suspected there was some trick with this hypnosis business: serenity is never free, you have to give something in exchange, and the clever old man had succeeded in extracting my secret.

"What's up, maestro?" Félix's loud greeting gave me a start just before I felt a slap on my back—why, I asked myself, did that runt have to show up precisely at that moment, just when I needed to be alone to sort out the consequences of my discovery? I had no choice but to maintain my composure, the worst thing would have been to expose my underbelly to my friend, a newsmonger of the first degree, who would broadcast any secret he heard through a megaphone. I told him they'd just given me my final check, and I was about to go buy my ticket, an excellent reason to be celebrating, and Félix quickly ordered a Bull, that sweet and explosive cocktail he was so wild about, and he ordered it loudly and accompanied by large gesticulations, because if there was anything Félix enjoyed, it was calling attention to himself, creating a brouhaha, especially when he'd had a little too much to drink, or when he was excited at the imminent prospect of treating his hangover, which was the case at that moment, because once he sat down on the stool it seemed like there were fire ants biting his butt, not just regular ones, like mine, that's how intensely agitated he was, his gestures so disproportional, his laughter so booming, that the bartender seemed nervous as he made his Bull, and the other two customers even whispered to each other and turned around to have a look. "*Salud!*" he shouted, banging his glass into mine then turning to the waiter and the other customers, as if he were the owner of the bar greeting his customers. He told me that the night before, he had been drinking till very late at the College, his favorite cantina on Amsterdam in Colonia Condesa, together with Aniceto, an old buddy from his days as a guerrilla commander, someone I'd had a few drinks with on a couple of occasions, enough for me to realize that this Aniceto guy was dangerous, or at least had been, proof of which was his guarded and circumspect demeanor, as if he didn't want anybody to discover he was there, exactly the opposite of my buddy Félix, who got people in trouble only by putting them in dubious situations with his temerity or his big mouth. I told him that the night before, I'd gotten plastered at my uncle's place—where I had taken him on more than one occasion—but I didn't mention the chase scene that fat-ass, Mario Varela, and I had acted out, not because I was ashamed but rather because of the risk that he would follow it up with a big song and dance, just to impress his audience, yelling about the stupidity of the Communists, appealing to the opinions of the bartender and the other customers, that was his style, and my nerves simply wouldn't be able to handle it. I also told him—lowering my voice to a whisper, like a conspirator asking for secrecy—the bad news about the disappearance of my doctor upon his arrival at the Comalapa Airport, a doctor I had already talked to Félix about during our get-togethers at La Veiga, but I had told him only that he was treating me for colitis, without mentioning then or now anything about acupuncture or hypnosis, because my friend would have pilloried me for believing in such practices, and he also would have wanted to get into an argument about it. "You're not getting cold feet, are you?" he asked, as if he could read in my face the dilemma I was in, whether I should take off right now to buy the ticket or wait till I heard news of Don Chente; and then he added, in a jocular tone, perhaps to quell fears also rising inside him, that most likely the old man had been drinking at the airport bar and the plane had left without him, an explanation that was so incongruent that I didn't even bother to refute it. He offered to accompany me to the travel agency after we'd gotten rid of our hangovers, because together we could more easily silence my consuming doubts, according to him, as if I were an imbecile and wholly unaware that his own fears stemmed from his own plans to return to our country and participate in the same magazine project, but it was in his interest that I go first, like the advance guard, or more like the slab of meat you throw to the stray dog to see if it still has teeth. I told him I had to go take a piss, which I proceeded to do, but before entering the restroom I stopped at the public telephone to call Muñecón, who again didn't answer, which further heightened my concerns, so after peeing I stood for a long time in front of the mirror over the sink with the tap running and asked myself, in a flash of lucidity, what the hell I was doing at that time of day getting drunk again with Félix, when I should have been focusing all my energy on dealing with issues related to my trip that were still pending; the check again started to burn a hole in my shirt, and what with the number of thieves in that city, it was bad luck to walk around with a check, I warned myself, then immediately, my gaze lost in the stream of water, I again began to experience that strange state of mind that had come over me the night before at my uncle's apartment, a morose state of mind that put me at one remove from myself and was accompanied by a voice that resounded in my head and expressed uneasiness at my behavior, that told me that I should feel the same disdain for myself that I felt for Félix, because I was no stranger to the temerity I criticized so harshly in him. Fortunately, at that moment another customer came into the restroom, whereby the voice went silent and the morose mood broke, which frightened me, to be honest, because that same voice had preceded the catastrophe that had forced me to flee for my life from my uncle's apartment, so I quickly turned off the tap, dried my hands, and made my way back to the bar and the business at hand.

Having already finished off our Bloody Caesars and our Bulls, we were just starting in on our second round of vodka tonics, surrounded by the buzz coming from several other tables behind us that had since become occupied, when Félix started to tell me a story that Aniceto had told him the night before at The College, he said, and he did it without the shouting I mentioned earlier, instead adopting the demeanor of a clandestine militant, which made me feel exceedingly disinclined to listen because I assumed that he'd once again tell me a story he'd already told me several times, this being his trademark pathology, which I had discovered nine years before, the second time I'd ever laid eyes on him, when he told me the same story he had told me at our first encounter the day before, as if he had never told it, needless to say, a pathology that at the time I attributed to the tremendous fear the poor guy must have experienced as a result of having been forced to become an armed urban commando, when quite obviously he was not prepared for it, and also to the guilt he suffered because the military had come to his house to get him and killed his brother-in-law when they didn't find him, and that was the story he repeated over and over, the story that made him ill, how he had eluded a military raid and how they had gotten even by gunning down his brother-in-law. I flew into a fit of rage, had an urge to shout at him to shut his trap, to stop him from repeating that same idiotic blather, but fortunately it was a fit that remained invisible to those around me, which explains why I suggested instead that we go look for a place to eat, some place other than

Sanborns, which was only good for treating our hangovers, a real restaurant, that is, and that he should save the story Aniceto had told him for our new venue.

"Perfect," Félix said, gulping down his vodka tonic and pressing me to finish mine while stating enthusiastically that the moment he opened his eyes that morning with the hangover hammering at his temples and his guts churning, he'd told himself he'd love to eat some Argentinian beef and chorizo, a strange assertion that I attributed to his bravado, because one thing is a hangover and another hunger, and nobody with churning guts can dream about eating meat. But, in the end, every belly is a world unto itself, and we paid and stepped out onto Insurgentes on the corner of San Antonio then turned toward El Gran Bife, an Argentinian restaurant located a few blocks away, so close you could see it from the terrace of La Veiga. But once we were outside under the midday sun, I discovered that the drinks had made me feel so good that I'd passed from a hangover to a prelude to revelry, and I also discovered that Félix was planning to invite some other friends to join us at the restaurant, thereby turning the meal into an actual party, which is why he stopped to call María Lima, the editor of the magazine's international page, his boss, and a couple of other reporters; while he was inviting them to El Gran Bife from the telephone booth on the corner of Porfirio Díaz, my eyes were drawn to the windows of Muñecón's apartment—his building was barely thirty yards away—and then I remembered that I had taken the taxi to escape from Mario Varela at this very same corner in the wee hours of the dawn, a curious spatial coincidence, I told myself, a sign that I moved in a tiny circle in the most populated city on the planet. When Félix finished talking, it was my turn, but nobody picked up on the other end of the line, and I was so worried that I had an urge to go to the building to check and see if my uncle's car was in its parking space, because ringing the bell without calling first would have been inexcusably reckless. As it turned out, I didn't have the opportunity to go to Muñecón's building, for although I had leapt from a hangover to a prelude to revelry, Félix had leapt even higher and more quickly, so high that the demons of urgency were already nipping at his heels, and the whole time we were striding down the four blocks past Parque Hundido, my friend was telling me we had to hurry, his editor was bringing along a new reporter, a woman with an ass straight out of the movies, and he was shouting, flinging his hands around and tracing the shape of her ass in the air, the look on his face like a jackal drooling at the sight of a succulent piece of carrion. "Calm down, you moron, they're not going to get there before us," I said, wanting him to slow down, feeling ridiculous at that desperate trot, and the worst part was that I was starting to sweat, a thick sticky sweat, a warning that my kidneys had an urgent need for at least one glass of water. And then I asked myself what was going on with me, what the hell was I doing darting around in a frenzy in the wake created by Félix's agitation, instead of going to the bank to deposit my check, eating something quickly, then showing up at the travel agency to buy my ticket, which would have been the correct way to proceed, above and beyond whatever had happened to my doctor, above and beyond whatever faces went unseen and hearts (in this case, conspiracies) went unknown, as they say in Mexico, then I stopped, with the sensation that something in my mind had fallen into place. We were about a hundred yards from El Gran Bife, at the corner of Insurgentes and San Lorenzo, when I realized that San Lorenzo was precisely the street Don Chente lived on, just three blocks down.

"I'll see you at the restaurant. I'm going to go try to pick up a notebook I left at my doctor's," I blurted out, then started quickly down San Lorenzo like somebody fleeing from an imminent shootout. After a moment of confusion, my friend likewise acted hastily, perhaps fearing that my abrupt swerve was merely a strategy to sneak away, or perhaps he was incapable of spending a moment alone, unable to bear his own exaltation without somebody there to listen to him, though before he came running after me, he did lodge a protest: "We can go get it after lunch." But I was already on my way, unstoppable and not slacking my pace even slightly, still hoping he would not follow me; I told him that I wouldn't have time after we ate, I still had a lot to do for my trip, which from all points of view was true, as was also my desire to disappear, and the possibility of getting my hands on the notebook where Don Chente had written down my confessions did not seem that outlandish. "How the hell are you going to get your notebook if you just told me that the old man went to San Salvador!?" my friend demanded as he caught up with me in a last-ditch effort to stop me, insisting that we first go to the restaurant. "His wife or the maid will be there," I said, hurrying my steps, and I repeated that he didn't have to come with me, it would be better if he went straight to the restaurant to get a good table, and I would catch up with him there in no more than fifteen minutes. But the die was cast, there was no way I could extricate myself from Félix, who had now started to run sulkily after me, because the idea of laying my hands on Don Chente's notebook had invigorated me, and my energetic and determined pace contrasted with how sluggish I had been feeling just moments before. We soon crossed to the next block, my steps spurred on by the prospect of the imminent recovery of that notebook, which really did belong to me, because what was written in it were the secrets of my life, and if Don Chente had indeed disappeared, the most prudent thing was for that information to be in my hands, I didn't want to even imagine what would happen if that notebook fell, for example, into the claws of someone like Félix, I told myself, feeling a hint of shivers running up and down my spine, the mere possibility of such an occurrence making me shake my head and speed my steps up still further; until that moment I hadn't realized that my friend had been there alongside me the whole time, blabbing away about how, because of me, the girls would get to the restaurant and leave when they didn't find us there, about how I would be sorry for having thrown away such an opportunity. But by then we were standing in front of that elegant building, my attention now focused on the doorbell, and I felt master of the situation, confident of achieving my goal. And a few seconds later I heard through the intercom the same voice I'd heard on most of my other visits, the voice of the maid asking who was there and what I wanted. I told her I was Erasmo Aragón, Don Chente's patient, that she had answered the door for me on other occasions, surely she remembered me, didn't she? and that at my last appointment I had left a notebook in the doctor's office and that he, before leaving for San Salvador, had left me a message telling me that I could drop by to pick it up, he would leave it with his wife or with her. "His wife went with him," the maid said. What an ass I am, I admonished myself, why didn't I realize that the doctor had gone with his wife! "And nobody told me anything about any notebook," the maid added, sounding like she wanted to put an end to the conversation. "The doctor must have forgotten, he left in such a hurry and was so sad about Doña Rosita's death," I said quickly, trying to retake the initiative, even surprised that for once my memory had worked in my favor and allowed me to remember the name of Don Chente's mother, mentioned at Muñecón's place the night before. And then I asked her if she would let me come up to look for the notebook, surely it was on his desk, I would immediately recognize it. She remained quiet for a few seconds, perhaps uncertain, but then said that she was sorry, her orders were not to open the door to anybody. "So maybe, since you can't let me in, you could do me the favor of going to look for it and bringing it to me," I suggested, using one final ploy and without straying from my measured and polite tone, at the same time as I became aware that Félix was bringing his face up to the intercom, his face that was all puffy from the booze, his eyes glassy, evidence that his wires were already crossed and fizzling. "Do what we say!" he shouted to my great surprise, "and hurry up about it!" in that scornful tone used to give orders to dim-witted domestics, as if he were about to give her a whipping, before I could push him away, bringing my finger angrily to my lips to tell him to shut up, his outburst was about to render all my efforts in vain. "What? Who's there?" the maid asked, now quite disconcerted. "Open up, this is the police!" Félix shouted, already in a state of rapture, gesticulating at the intercom, while the urge to grab him by the hair and slam his face into the glass door came over me at the exact instant I clearly heard the click of the intercom as the maid hung up the phone, which only increased my rage because I understood that she had withdrawn in alarm, and if at first she had trusted me, she had now acted out of fear and suspicion. But Félix was infatuated by the role he was playing, and when he realized that the maid had hung up, he began ringing the doorbell compulsively, over and over again, his face contorted in rage, insulting her and threatening her, as if she were still listening to him, his behavior so scandalous that I feared the neighbors would come out and give us a piece of their mind, so I began to retreat to the sidewalk, my head down, my rage turning into chagrin at the pathetic spectacle my friend was making of himself, and I managed to say, "Let's go, you moron, you already fucked everything up."

We walked down San Lorenzo back toward Insurgentes, my buddy Félix still shouting behind me about how could "that goddamn half-breed" possibly have refused to return my notebook to me, whereas I was being pulled in different directions by insidious emotions, on the one hand wanting to skewer my companion, tell him to get lost, go to hell, leave me alone, and on the other hand blaming myself: I was the only one to blame for what had happened to me because I was the one who had invited Félix to meet me at Sanborns instead of nursing my hangover alone and then going to deposit my check and buying my airplane ticket, which would have been the commonsensical thing to do; but instead, I'd had the brilliant idea of calling my buddy Félix and not somebody else. And so we continued, together but each in his own world, and when we turned down a side street, I heard a voice behind me calling out, "Young men!" a voice I immediately turned toward only to find that it came from a couple of policemen in a patrol car driving slowly behind us, as if they were escorting us, or checking us out. "Stop!" the fat one with the porcine nose sitting behind the steering wheel shouted, pulling the car over to the curb and starting to open the door, an order in response to which my first impulse was to take off running, as fast as my legs could carry me, a normal reaction for someone from the country I was from, and therefore also normal for Félix, whose face underwent an abrupt transformation due to the same combustion that was taking place inside me and that burned off the last drop of alcohol in my bloodstream—we'd been caught completely unawares, my companion in the middle of his harangue and me in my bewilderment; so, after that initial blast of fear, we just stood there stock still and waited for the officers to reach us, the fat one with the porcine nose and a skinny short one with a mustache like Cantinflas, who asked us point-blank: "What's going on, why are you making such a fuss so early in the morning?" And he barked that in a tone of voice somewhere between cunning and ass-licking, like a dog playing with his prey before biting into it. "What fuss?" Félix answered, having abruptly pulled himself together and adopted a certain aloofness toward the men in uniform standing in front of us—these were not ghoulish Salvadoran soldiers but rather mooching, mud-brained Mexican policemen. But the fat one with the porcine nose rudely answered that we had been threatening people in the building back there, and we had to accompany them to the station, and—now in a rather intimidating tone that made his nostrils flare and vibrate—he demanded that we show him our IDs, whereat my friend haughtily pulled out his wallet to show them his press credentials, on the corner of which shone the logo of the magazine he worked for, which immediately deflated the fat one and also the little guy with the mustache like Cantinflas—before they were snarling and snapping their jaws but now they were all bark and no bite. And while my buddy Félix was explaining to them that the whole mess was because that dirty little maid didn't want to give me back my notebook that I had left in my doctor's apartment, I stood there in a state of suspension, at first terrified at the possibility that the policemen would make us get into their patrol car and would find my final paycheck in my pocket, then with a strong urge to tell them that Félix was lying, that he and not the maid had been the cause of everything, that only he would have had the bright idea to shout insults and threats through an intercom at a girl who was only following orders, and would they please do me the favor of arresting him and taking him to the station without further delay. But instead of that, I somewhat abashedly held out my press credentials, feeling as if I were lying, knowing

I was the only one to blame for the whole fiasco, for hanging out with the people I hung out with instead of making my way alone, but all they needed was one glance at my credentials, issued by the news agency I no longer worked for, to be fully convinced that they weren't going to get enough money out of us for a soda pop, at which point they told us to continue along our way, they even addressed us as "gentlemen," before returning to their car.

"Dumbass scum," Félix exclaimed, made a contemptuous gesture once the patrol car had disappeared down Fresas Street, and then immediately let out a defiant shout: "What the fuuuuck, you motherfuckers!" while flinging his arms into the air as if in celebration, like a gladiator who has just claimed victory over his most ferocious opponent, just as I became aware that I was bathed in sweat, so much so that I had to take off my jacket because my shirt was soaked under my armpits. "Your own damn fault, you moron," I managed to say to my friend in reproach, but he was no longer paying any attention to me, he was rushing forward, now with renewed energy, and rushing me, telling me how those women with their fine asses were probably about to arrive at the restaurant, if they hadn't already, and rubbing his hands together with glee. The fact that I was feeling like I was coming apart at the seams because my moods had been swinging back and forth on a crazy pendulum would have been obvious to anyone who saw me walking behind my buddy Félix on my way to El Gran Bife, looking disheveled, my mind in even more of a tangle, until suddenly I recalled what the maid had said, that Don Chente had flown to El Salvador with his wife, which made it well-nigh impossible that they had taken him captive, she was a member of the oligarchy, and he was an old man and not a member of any party whatsoever; so, at the door to the restaurant, I told my friend that I had to call Muñecón again and dashed off to the phone booth on the corner, where I finally managed to get a hold of my uncle, whom I eagerly asked if my doctor had ever shown up. "Yeah, why?" he asked me, just as calmly as could be, as if he hadn't been the one who had told me of his disappearance, and it wasn't till that moment that I realized that my uncle was probably suffering from a worse hangover than mine, if he was not still intoxicated, but instead of asking for explanations or recriminating him for throwing me into a maelstrom, I felt enormous relief, as if in one fell swoop all the loose pieces inside me had fallen into place. I stood for a few seconds with the phone glued to my ear, not saying anything, contemplating Félix at the doorway of the restaurant pointing to the table where he would wait for me, while out of the corner of my eye I glimpsed, at the corner of Insurgentes and Félix Cuevas, the bank where I should have gone hours earlier.

11

AND THERE I WAS, sitting at the small bar, where I could see
Gate 19, a can of Tecate beer in my hand, trying to control my
nervousness, which was threatening to overwhelm me, because
I was about to finally embark on my trip of return, in one hour
at the most I would board the airplane that would carry me to a
new phase in my life, to confront the challenge of reinventing myself under conditions of constant, daily danger, where I would be
forced to remain lucid and would learn to have control over how
I spent my energy, which I was looking forward to; to achieve
this, I counted on meeting, at least once more, Don Chente, the
doctor who would give me clues to myself, whose revelations
would guide me toward a longed-for equilibrium. In the mean-
time, however, I was extremely thirsty, the past few days I'd been
living at a million miles a minute, clearing away all kinds of ob-
stacles, especially trying to calm down Eva, whose emotional in-
stability continued to increase as the day of my departure approached; the night before, I had barely been able to sleep at all
precisely because of how upset she was, because she reproached

me again and again for abandoning them, for fleeing like a coward from my paternal responsibilities, for choosing to go run after some stupid danger rather than make an effort to repair our relationship. It didn't do any good for me to reassure her that she would receive her monthly stipend for our daughter's upkeep, that every three months I'd return to Mexico so as not to lose my residence permit, that at the slightest inkling of a threat from the army I would return without delay; it did no good for me to beg her to let me sleep a little, even once we were lying in bed with the lights off, she started up again with her tears and exclamations, until she woke up Evita, and the poor girl ended up climbing into our bed, something we had already gotten her out of the habit of doing, and even though at a certain point I thought about going downstairs to sleep on the sofa in the living room, I didn't have the strength to do it, trapped as I was in that morose state of mind, a result of the guilt Eva had infected me with. And if that wasn't enough, and in spite of my pleas to the contrary, she insisted on driving me to the airport in the morning with Evita, her heart set on acting out a melodramatic farewell à la Mexican soap opera, as if she didn't know that I've always hated goodbyes, that tears and pseudo-sentimental smooching disgust me, that even at parties I try to leave without anybody noticing, I slip away at the slightest excuse, I really do, I'm so impatient I can't tolerate people who spend hours and hours saying goodbye, as if they were at an eternal dinner party, which is why I insisted that we say goodbye at home and that I take a taxi to the airport; in addition, flying makes me anxious, which then affects my nervous system, and I become prey to uncontrollable irritability. But she didn't listen to my arguments, and after I checked in, when the only thing I wanted to do was go through immigration and get to the gate, she suggested we go have something to drink, because I still had plenty of time, she said, and Evita seconded her, she also wanted a refreshment, the girl said, haltingly, and I had no choice but to accompany them to Bar Morado, where I drank my first beer of the day while Eva repeated her refrain from the night before, and I tried to disconnect, to listen to her without hearing as my mind sought refuge in the imminent future, repeating to myself that once I got to San Salvador, I'd make drastic changes in my life, like taking up exercise and abstaining from alcohol, even if at that moment I needed the beer I was drinking to calm me down, until she said something she had not yet said, and her tone of voice was harsh when she muttered it: that my obsession with returning to San Salvador now that the war was about to end was a way of hiding my cowardice, and by so doing I was trying to cover up the fact that during the war I had never had the courage to fight with the guerrillas, as my friends had done, and that instead I had spent my time boasting and drinking, and now that there was no longer any danger because the war was coming to an end and nobody cared about me, I wanted to return and pretend I was brave, make a big fanfare out of my courage, when in fact what I was perpetuating was a new form of cowardice by not accepting my responsibilities. I was so full of rage that I didn't open my mouth, I just stared at her with the most abject hatred, repeating to myself that it wasn't worth responding, that with that accusation she had shut all the doors, and any response from me would plunge us into a futile argument in front of the child. I drank down the rest of my beer, then went to pay and get the goodbyes over with, because as soon as possible I wanted to escape Eva's new bout of tears, her mixture of resentment and scorn, and also the expression of alarm on Evita's face, which I was kissing in an attempt to communicate to her a false sense of joy and serenity, as if nothing were going on, as if her mother's tears weren't what they seemed to be, then waving my hand and making loving faces at my daughter as I lined up to go through security, with a heaviness in my chest that did not leave me from that moment on, not while I was being screened, not when I waved goodbye one last time to the two Evas, not when I handed my passport over to the immigration officer, not even when I passed through the duty-free stores and checked out the price of vodka, unable to decide when faced with a tempting deal—a half gallon of Finlandia at bargain-basement prices—because one part of me refused to go past the duty-free shops without taking advantage of their bargains, while the other part of me, a pretty rickety one, why deny it, was telling me that if I really intended to start a new life, the least sensible thing for me to do would be to buy a half-gallon of vodka, which would only sink me deep into the same old rut. I resolved my dilemma in a flash of Solomonic wisdom after spending nearly ten minutes among the bottle-laden shelves: I would buy the half gallon, not for myself but as a gift for the friends I would be staying with that first week while I looked for an apartment.

And there I was, leaning on my elbows on the small bar in a corner of the waiting area, listening carefully for announcements about Gate 19 over the loudspeakers, drinking my second beer of the day, my duty-free bag at my feet next to my carry-on suitcase, watching the other passengers, looking to see if I recognized anybody, because most of the flights to Central America left from this gate, and it wouldn't have surprised me to see a familiar face: a journalist colleague, a politician anxious to talk to the press, or a guerrilla fighter dressed up as a businessman. But at that moment, fortune pointed elsewhere, in the direction of a thoroughbred filly who made me shake my head and gulp down my beer—and what a woman she was—a brunette with long legs scantily covered by a miniskirt, and a round upturned ass that at that very moment was settling delicately down into a chair while she gave instructions to a couple of kids, who appeared to be hers and who were struggling with carry-on bags of their own. A vision of such splendor produced a blast of desire so powerful that my throat immediately got parched, whereby I turned to the bartender and asked him to make me a vodka tonic, but he failed to respond, also dazzled by the sight of the brunette, until I tapped on the bar and winked at him; the guy responded with a whistle of admiration, and while he was mixing my drink, I turned to look again at the bombshell, who was now browsing a fashion magazine, indifferent to all the eyes browsing her, and then probably because of all the last day's ups and downs, I found myself comparing the woman I was looking at there in front of me to the woman I had just abandoned, because Eva was also a brunette and also had the kind of body that soaked up men's libidinous stares, but she was about four inches shorter than this filly, which made her legs, though beautiful, less conspicuous, and along this same route of comparative analysis I remembered a sentence Eva had dumped on me the night before and had then whispered again in my ear as we were saying goodbye in front of security: "Stop running away from your paternity; your daughter is waiting for you," or something like that, as if she were some hotshot psychoanalyst and had just reinvented the wheel, as if it hadn't been me who had explained to her that the contempt that my grandmother Lena had inculcated in me for my father was what made difficult not only my own paternity but who knows what other aspects of my life. But I had also explained to her several times that seeing clearly the source of an illness didn't mean that the illness would cease to exist, one also needed to repair what had been destroyed; I had even given her some examples: ultimately we are like a machine, I told her, and seeing in the bright light of high noon that the carburetor is broken doesn't solve anything, you need a mechanic who knows how to take out the bad carburetor and install a new one. That, I told her, was why it was so important for me to continue undergoing treatment with Don Chente, because he alone knew the convolutions of the dark side of my being and could help me find clues that would allow me to shed light on it, because that was what it was all about, shedding light on the dark side, as the old man himself had explained to me in more than one session; that, I told her, was why it was a happy coincidence that my doctor was now in San Salvador, because I would have the possibility of continuing the treatment even if only for a short time, because Muñecón had reassured me that Don Chente was planning to stay there for a couple of weeks and had given me a telephone number where I could reach him, I remembered, patting my chest over the inside pocket of my jacket, where I kept my datebook.

The brunette stood up, put the magazine down on her chair, and bent over to look through her carry-on bag—her miniskirt edged up, more generously exposing her thighs—while scolding the children who weren't paying any attention to her. The bartender and I, as well as probably half the waiting room, were holding our breaths, as if on tenterhooks, the scene seemingly frozen into an abrupt silence while she continued to look through her bag, her buttocks in the air, until she straightened up, smoothed down her miniskirt, went back to her chair, picked up her magazine, and began reading. I took a big sip of vodka to celebrate, convinced now that she was Salvadoran and that I would have a chance to talk to her during the flight, even the fantasy of having a woman like that when I arrived in San Salvador was enough to change my mood, and whereas before I'd been hearing a soundtrack of the irritating squawks of my argument with Eva, now an intoxicating melody was playing, because, the fact was, ever since I had gone through immigration, I had entered a new state, bachelorhood—hurrah!—and a paradise full of sweet asses awaited me at my destination, of course not all of them like this filly's, the sight of which I was now so greatly enjoying, but a paradise nonetheless, a prospect that made me ecstatic and sent me into a trance ... But what if she wasn't on her way to El Salvador? I asked myself as I drank down the last of my vodka tonic. And what if she was traveling with the children's father? ... I convinced myself that I should approach her now or never, and armed as I was with the audacity a few drinks can provide, pulling behind me my rolling suitcase and carrying the duty-free bag in my other hand, I gallantly started off in the direction of the row of seats where she was reading, then without preamble I asked her if the seat next to hers was free: she looked up at me, slightly put out, and without saying a word indicated that I could sit there if I wanted; but at that instant and out of the blue, one of her boys climbed onto the chair and pronounced it taken. I stood there stunned for a few seconds, looking at his fat little face and insolent grin, then managed to eke out a nervous little laugh, like an idiot on show in front of everybody in the waiting room, especially the bartender, who had sent me off with a wink of complicity. She didn't lift her eyes from the magazine, as if the whole scene had left her wholly indifferent, and I, having already lost my nerve, immediately looked for a place to sit down in the row of seats facing her, trying to conceal my confusion but not knowing how to occupy my mind and my hands, above all my mind, which was now reproaching me for my inability to react, because what I should have done was take advantage of the kid's effrontery to strike up a conversation, ask her questions about her children, and in that way find my way forward; and I felt intense hatred toward that fat little boy I was now looking at with the sullen expression of a tolerant adult, to which he responded with another insolent look. And then I turned back to the woman, who was barely five feet away from me, and I realized that the whole time she had been aware of the situation and was definitely amused at my expense, no matter how serious or how focused on the magazine she looked, at any moment it would become impossible for her to contain herself and a smile would betray her, that's why I didn't take my eyes off her; and I even allowed myself to look down at her thighs covered with delicate golden fuzz, a sight that was very nearly driving me crazy, nothing excites me more than a lower back or thighs covered with delicate golden fuzz; but the person who was really going crazy was the boy in the chair, because when he realized that I was looking at his mother's thighs, he leapt up, his face twisted in rage, and threw himself against the other boy, who was sitting on the ground leaning on the carry-on bag, locking arms with him in a wrestling match that had them both rolling around on the tiled floor. The brunette called them to order with a threat, but she didn't stand up or look at me again. And then I asked myself whether Evita reacted that violently when a strange man approached her mother, a question that only proceeded to sink me deeper into sadness, because suddenly I realized how voluble my character was, the way events could do with me whatever they wanted, so that instead of remaining lucid as I stood on the brink of this new stage of my life, there I was, getting seriously unhinged, drooling like an idiot at the sight of a stranger, my ego battered, thrashed by a child. Damn, all I needed now was a bout of self-mortification . . .

Fortunately, at that very moment, the door at Gate 19 opened for the passengers who had just arrived on the flight from San

Salvador, according to the announcement over the loudspeaker made by an airline employee, who requested that we remain alert, we would begin boarding in about fifteen minutes. I looked up to see if I recognized any of the arriving passengers and observed the agitated expressions on their faces, some of whom were confused about which way to go for immigration and customs, but I didn't recognize anybody, and a few minutes later I saw the brunette stand up, exclaim in delight, and walk over to a woman who had just disembarked, a woman she embraced effusively right next to me, allowing me to contemplate—enthralled—her thighs and ass, within reach of my hand, which I didn't dare move, just to be clear, because I sat absolutely still in my privileged position, like a chameleon invisibly perched on his branch, because I did not want them to be aware of my presence, not for anything in the world, not while I was furtively and ecstatically contemplating the edges of her olive-skinned glutes, also covered in delicate golden fuzz—damn, a spasm of desire was shaking me to the core—until the boy mentioned earlier appeared and positioned himself defiantly and with furrowed brow between my gaze and his mother's backside at the very moment she turned to tell him to say hello to the woman she had been embracing. That was when I turned and looked in the opposite direction, where the recently arrived passengers were moving toward customs and immigration, and I even stood up, turning my back on her, afraid that the kid would snitch on me, tell her I was ogling her, but also seized with a certain uneasiness, because now I knew that the brunette would be on my flight and the contemplation of her silky flesh had befuddled my senses, to the extent that I was not even paying attention to the arriving passengers, as if my entire being had remained glued to the skin on the backs of her thighs leading up to her glutes. And because my mind had been rendered much too vulnerable by all those impressions and emotions, I suddenly found myself wondering where it came from, all that anxiety that overwhelmed me whenever I spotted a pair of beautiful legs under a miniskirt, anxiety that obliged me to look at those legs compulsively, like a voyeur, no matter what the circumstances, a kind of vice or obsession that had accompanied me since my early adolescence, since the awakening of my sexuality, and that had always driven crazy the women who had shared their lives with me. And then an image rose out of my memory: during my first years of high school at the all-boys school run by Marist priests where I was a student, a group of boys would gather every afternoon on a kind of embankment under which passed cars driven by young mothers taking their children to school or picking them up and from which we could catch a clear glimpse, under the steering wheels, of the naked thighs of the drivers who were wearing miniskirts, thighs that excited us, made us shout out in delight, and supplied us with images for our masturbations. Needless to say, not one of the mothers of the members of that group drove under that embankment where we stood to get a peek into those cars, and even if one had, she would not have been an object of interest, our mothers belonged to an older generation, one that didn't wear miniskirts, and the women who awoke our incipient lechery were younger women who were taking their children to nursery school or primary school. And while I stared distractedly at the crowd in the opposite direction from the brunette with the spectacular legs, I told myself that even if my mother had worn a miniskirt, she never would have awoken my interest, that I had never felt the least bit attracted to her, on the contrary, my grandmother Lena had taken it upon herself to revile her so much that she'd made mincemeat of my Oedipus complex from a very tender age ...

It was then that I thought I saw someone I knew among the crowd that was making its way into customs, not a face, because I was seeing their backs, but rather a way of walking, of moving down the corridor, but at that instant I couldn't make out who it might be, so I picked up my duty-free bag and grabbed the handle of my carry-on suitcase so that I could walk around a little to quell the agitation the sight of the brunette and the thoughts derived thereof had caused me, and also to get another glimpse at the person whose way of walking had seemed so familiar. And that was when it came to me in a flash: Holy shit! It was Don Chente, my doctor! I walked quickly toward customs, where the recent arrivals were lining up to have their passports checked and where two health officials were questioning them about the countries they had visited, and I made my way with some difficulty through the crowd of passengers bunching up together in that corridor, apologizing because my carry-on suitcase and my duty-free bag kept banging into people, but by the time I reached the counter, Don Chente had already passed through, and those who were still waiting were shouting at me, thinking that I wanted to cut the line and sneak in ahead of them, and one of the officials stopped me and ordered me to get to the end of the line, to show some respect, to which I responded that I hadn't just arrived, I was waiting to depart but had seen my doctor disembark, and I urgently needed to talk to him, would he please let me pass, but I begged in vain, because the official told me that only arriving passengers could go past that point, nobody else, that was the regulation, while I was straining my neck, trying to get a glimpse of Don Chente, whom I thought I saw next to a posh woman about to have her passport checked, but then I lost him in the crowd, and the health officer repeated, now even more rudely, that I needed to leave, I was in the way. Aghast and dumbstruck, I stood to one side of the entryway, holding on to my duty-free bag and my carry-on suitcase, looking at the anxious faces surrounding me, some apparently angry and with a curse on the tips of their tongues, until finally, at the other end of Gate 19, I saw the brunette saying goodbye to her friend who had just arrived, and I hastily turned my steps in that direction, lurching against the strong current of passengers streaming the other way, knowing that she alone would listen intently to all my woes.